C0-AWC-948

A COOL, CLEAR DEATH

A Cool, Clear Death

Tucker Halleran

ST. MARTIN'S PRESS/NEW YORK

Triskidekaphobia is the irrational fear of all things
pertaining to the number thirteen. That's why there
isn't a chapter thirteen in this book. With apologies to
all logic enthusiasts and with thanks to an indulgent
publisher.

—Tucker Halleran

A COOL, CLEAR DEATH. Copyright © 1984 by Tucker Halleran. All rights
reserved. Printed in the United States of America. No part of this book
may be used or reproduced in any manner whatsoever without written
permission except in the case of brief quotations embodied in critical
articles or reviews. For information, address St. Martin's Press, 175 Fifth
Avenue, New York, N.Y. 10010.

Design by Manny Paul

Library of Congress Cataloging in Publication Data
Halleran, Tucker.
    A cool, clear death.
    I. Title.
PS3558.A3795C6   1984   813'.54   84-13260
ISBN 0-312-16954-X

First Edition

10 9 8 7 6 5 4 3 2 1

To Judy—who kept the faith

It is—last stage of all—
When we are frozen up within and quite
The phantom of ourselves,
To hear the world applaud the hollow ghost,
Which blamed the living man.

—Matthew Arnold
"Growing Old"

A Cool,
Clear
Death

1

Form 447-380

POLICE DEPARTMENT
CITY OF CYPRESS BEACH, FLORIDA

DATE: December 13, 1981   **CASE NUMBER: CB-347-41**
TIME: 10:18 P.M.   **SUPERVISOR:** Lt. W. Hampton
                                   INVESTIGATING
                                   OFFICER (S):
                                      Sgt. D Serkin
                                      Off. J. Randolph

SUBJECT: Homicide—*Morgan,* Laura E., Mrs.

REMARKS: Statement of Mr. Ralph Morgan, husband of deceased. Witnessed by Lt. W. Hampton, Sgt. D. Serkin, Off. J. Randolph

Q. You are Mr. Ralph Morgan, husband of the deceased, Mrs. Laura Morgan?
A. Laura Evans Morgan. Yes, sir, I am.
Q. You have been advised of your rights, Mr. Morgan. Do you understand them?

1

A. Yes, I do.

Q. Specifically, you have the right to have an attorney present at this time. You understand that?

A. Yes. I don't want an attorney. I just want you to get whoever did this. You have to find out why they did this, please.

Q. Very well, Mr. Morgan. Let the record show Mr. Morgan voluntarily waived his rights to have an attorney present. Now, Mr. Morgan, please give us your account of this incident, including your whereabouts from the last time you saw the deceased alive until you spoke to the investigating officers.

A. All right. I'll try, but I'm so confused. Please. It's all such a horrible shock. What, where should I start?

Q. Take your time, Mr. Morgan. Try to be as specific as you can. When did you last see your wife?

A. The last time I saw Laura was when I was leaving for work. I went in the bedroom to try to say good-bye.

Q. Did you say "try," Mr. Morgan?

A. Yes. She wasn't speaking to me. We'd had a big argument. You know how it is. She didn't answer me, just rolled over in bed with her back to me. I was so upset I stormed out. Even left my briefcase behind with an investment model I had developed over the weekend and wanted to send to the home office.

Q. Please try to stick to the pertinent facts, Mr. Morgan. About what time was that?

A. Sorry. A little before eight. I like to get to the office by eight-thirty. It's about a twenty-minute drive, usually, but I always allow for delays. I got there about eight-thirty, as usual. Mrs. Stauder, my secretary, was there when I arrived. I spent the morning on the telephone. Mondays are terrible. I'm a stockbroker and clients get a lot of half-baked ideas over the weekend, have to call you first thing to check them out. Then, I went to lunch. I guess it was a little after one. I got a sandwich at the deli and went to the park near the beach.

Q. Do you customarily have lunch alone, Mr. Morgan?

A. No, I don't. Not usually. Usually, I'm with a customer, but I was still upset about our quarrel; I just wanted time to think things out. See how we could make up. I really hate it when she doesn't speak. You know? I can't handle that. When I got back to the office it was about two-fifteen. I went to the partners' meeting at two-thirty. We have one every Monday. I spent the rest of the day trying to drum up some business. The stock market has been so slow lately, ever since November. I'm afraid if I don't get some heavy action pretty soon we may have to start digging into savings. That won't go over very well at home. What am I saying? Sorry. I'm sorry. I'll be all right. I was just finishing up some paperwork when my telephone rang. Mrs. Stauder didn't answer it, so it must have been after five. Laura was on the phone. Said she'd gotten a call from a man named Anderson, friend of a client of mine, Carl Ballantine.

Q. Are you acquainted with this Mr. Anderson, Mr. Morgan?

A. No. Never heard of him before. Laura said he was quite anxious to talk to me. She said he was leaving for a two-month stay in Europe and didn't want to let his investment portfolio slide for that long. He suggested we meet at a restaurant in Boca Raton called Palminteri's. Said he'd make a reservation in his name at eight. Laura told him she thought that would be all right with me, then called to tell me.

Q. Isn't that somewhat unusual, Mr. Morgan?

A. No. Not really. We're like realtors and insurance agents: we do a lot of business at night and on weekends, a great deal of it in restaurant meetings. I *was* annoyed, though. I mean it required going home to get my model and some other stuff in my briefcase, then another twenty-minute drive north to find a restaurant I'd never been to. Finally, back home to deal with Laura's lousy mood. Oh, God.

Q. Take your time, Mr. Morgan. So you were annoyed at having to meet this Mr. Anderson?

A. Yes, I guess annoyed is putting it mildly. Still the market is terrible and Laura was right, the man sounded like a good prospect, maybe even an immediate one. So, I got the directions from her, asked her to put my briefcase in the front hall, hung up, and began putting together a package for him. My personal credentials and some recommendations on various investments—you know, long- versus short-term gains, degree of risk versus return, common stock or preferred, bonds, money market funds, that kind of thing. I didn't know what he was looking for. Worked up to about six-thirty. Then I left to go home to get the briefcase.

Q. Who else was in the office when you left, Mr. Morgan?

A. No one. I remember having locked up myself. I'm often the last one to leave. I got home, called out to Laura. She didn't answer me. The bag was in the front hall, though, as I'd asked. So, I picked it up and left.

Q. Any feeling for what time it was?

A. I think around seven. I'd come straight home from the office. Usually takes about that long.

Q. Did you see anyone at that time, Mr. Morgan? Anyone see you? Like neighbors?

A. Not that I recall, but you must realize I was most distracted. My wife wasn't speaking to me, I had to go to a strange restaurant and try to sell a man I'd never met. Surely, you understand I . . . could we stop for a minute? I need a drink of water in the worst way.

Q. Of course, Mr. Morgan. Randolph, a glass of water for Mr. Morgan, please.

A. Thank you, I'm . . . most grateful. Where were we now?

Q. On your way to the restaurant, Mr. Morgan.

A. Right. Laura's directions said number 3400 West Palmetto Park Road in Boca. Three miles from I-95, on the right. She said the number was important because Anderson told her the restaurant was set back from the road and not very well lit.

Q. Approximately what time did you arrive at this Palminteri's, Mr. Morgan?

A. That's what's so crazy. I looked for it all the way to Route 441. I turned around there and went back, looking across the traffic to try to spot it. Nothing. By then it was almost eight and I was getting nervous. I figured Anderson would think I was rude for being late and pretty stupid for not being able to find a public restaurant. So, I turned around again. Only this time I decided to play it really safe. When I'd gone two miles, I pulled over, got my flashlight out of the glove compartment, and went on. I got over on the right as far as I could, drove as slowly as I could, using the flashlight to pick out the numbers. That's when I saw the sign.

Q. For the restaurant? Palminteri's?

A. No. It was a big white wooden sign in the middle of a field. I stopped and got out to make sure. The sign said they were opening a new K-Mart there in August—3200–3600 West Palmetto Park Road.

Q. Make a mistake taking down the directions, Mr. Morgan?

A. Well, that's what I thought. But I went through all my pockets and finally found the buck slip I wrote them on. I shined the flashlight on it. It said number 3400 all right. I thought maybe Laura blew it. So, I figured I'd better call her and find out.

Q. What was the answer?

A. There wasn't any. The phone kept ringing and ringing, so I gave up. Laura always takes a bath around then, and when she gets in the tub with the water running, you can hold a parade through the living room and she'll never know.

Q. Go on, Mr. Morgan.

A. I decided to find out where Palminteri's really was, so I could call Anderson and apologize for the mix-up. You know, so maybe we could still get together, later or when he got back from Europe. So, I called directory assistance and found out from the operator that there wasn't any Palminteri's Restaurant. Not in Boca, or Delray, or Cypress Beach, or Deerfield, or Pompano, or Fort Lauderdale. I spelled it out for the operator three times. No dice, even under new listings.

Q. What did you do at that point, Mr. Morgan?

A. There was nothing left to do but go home. Chalk it up as the perfect ending for a lousy day. I remember thinking that if this turned out to be a practical joke, Anderson must be some kind of a louse. I have to call Ballantine and find out, get to the bottom—I can't—I just can't believe this.

Q. Go on, Mr. Morgan, please. What did you do then?

A. I went home. I parked the car in our slot and went into the house. I yelled to Laura that I was home. I didn't get any answer, so I figured she was probably in the tub. Or that she still wasn't speaking to me. Either way, I remember I wanted a nice strong Scotch. So, I made a drink and went upstairs. And . . . and . . . that's when I found Laura. Dead on the bed. She was naked, with a bathrobe sash pulled around her neck. Oh, God. Her face was purple. Her tongue was sticking out. It was horrible. I knew she was dead. I knew the minute I saw her. I knew it.

Q. It's okay, Mr. Morgan. Tell us what happened next. Please be as specific as you can, Mr. Morgan. Mr. Morgan?

A. What? Oh, right. Look, I was shocked. Totally. Scared. I remember thinking I had to get out. That whoever did it might still be there. I ran downstairs, threw the door open, and ran outside. It was so quiet. Nobody was outside. Everybody at home. Then I . . . I went back in; my heart felt like it was exploding. I got the poker from the fireplace. I started walking through the first-floor rooms.

I opened the closets. No one. I went upstairs again. I was holding my breath, listening for any noise. I think I went into the den first, then the guest room and the bathroom; anyway, I checked them. I was absolutely terrified. But I didn't find anything or anybody. I had to force myself to go back into the master bedroom. I tried not to look at Laura's bod—May I stop a minute. Please. I . . .

Q. Easy, Mr. Morgan, we're in no hurry. You went into the bedroom. Then what?

A. I'm trying to remember. Oh, yes. That was it. The big framed picture she has of her brother. It was lying on the floor, smashed. I know I wasn't thinking straight because I figured she must have really been upset with me to throw that. She treasured that picture. Then, I guess, that's when the whole thing registered. And I . . . I started crying.

Q. Was that about the time you called us?

A. Yes, I know I should have done it right away. I know that. But I was so stunned and frightened I guess I wasn't thinking very well. I'm sorry. The man on the phone told me to stay put, not to touch anything. He said they would send a patrol car as soon as possible. I covered Laura with her bathrobe. I didn't want anyone to look at her like that. Maybe I shouldn't have. I don't know. All I wanted to do was cover her. She looked so cold.

Q. Continue, please, Mr. Morgan. What did you do next?

A. I went downstairs and waited until these two officers arrived.

Q. Anything to add to this statement, Mr. Morgan? Take your time, please; it's quite important.

A. No. No. That's all. That's all I can remember. Can I go home now? I have to see about Laura.

Q. I'm afraid not, Mr. Morgan. In the first place, your apartment is sealed off and will stay that way until the Crime Scene Squad and the Homicide people are done with it. We'll send someone over tomorrow for your personal effects. Don't worry about Mrs. Morgan. We'll take care of all that. Now, if you will go with Sergeant Serkin.

A. What do you mean? Hey, wait a . . . Do you think I? That I? Didn't—I didn't. She's my wife. Laura's my wife. I love her. You can't think . . .

Q. Mr. Morgan, as of now you aren't accused of anything. But surely you realize your statement raises quite a few serious questions. I'm afraid we'll have to bind you over until we get answers to these questions. Starting tomorrow, after you've had a chance to rest. And, Mr. Morgan, I advise you in the strongest possible terms to have counsel present with you then.

A. Oh, my God. Laura.

END TRANSCRIPT
11:26 P.M.

2

The wind woke me, moving the curtains aside, bringing with it the rich smell of the sea and the sounds of rigging slatting against the masts of the boats moored along the canal. When I first moved to Lighthouse Point that sound had irritated me, but now it's a welcome part of living on the waterfront, a reassurance that the boats are home and all is well.

I flipped the covers back, swung out of bed, and limped over to the picture window to see what sort of a day South Florida had brought me. The limp is a persistent reminder of another existence, in a much less civilized environment, where linebackers and other sadists periodically tried separating me from my intellect. They never succeeded, despite what some of my more envious friends say, but they got enough of the knee to make the going stiff in the morning and throughout the rainy season. Rah, rah, rah to you, too.

The twinge was worse than usual this morning, making me think we were in for some unexpected December rain, at least unexpected by the expert on Channel 5, who had said confidently last night that we could expect a clear, cool day, with no small-craft advisories.

Based on that information I'd called Ollie Morse—actually Adm. Oliver Hazzard Morse, U.S.N., Ret.—to propose another round in our ongoing attempt to reduce the pompano population of South Florida. On the surface that sounds cruel, but we think of it as a public service. There are a lot more pompano than people, and if public-spirited citizens didn't take action, we'd be up to our hips in pompano. Besides which, they make lovely eating and a day on the water with the Admiral is a thing to be treasured. Ollie is seventy-eight and his eyesight is going, but he has the best nose for pompano from here to Key West. He is also a world-class yarn spinner, not all the way back to the days of wooden ships and iron men, but pretty close. If you said, "Ollie, tell me again about fighting the pirates on the Yangtze River," you were guaranteed three hours of wall-to-wall swashbuckling. Long ago I'd given up trying to separate fact from fiction and simply gave way to the enjoyment of examining the verbal pictures he painted and the language his wife would never permit ashore.

This morning, the twinge in the knee and the wind that woke me pointed to a postponement of fishing activity in a small boat, and I cursed the Channel 5 man and all of his kind. I have a theory about weathermen—or meteorologists as today's types choose to label themselves—which says, the degree of probability of a weatherman's forecast varies in inverse proportion to the sophistication of his equipment. Put another way, show me a polyestered smirker with aerial photographs, sliding maps, and color radar and I'll show you a guy I'm not taking to the dog track.

The pity is, there's a much simpler way. If you really want to know what the weather is going to do, just call me and say, "Cam, how's the knee?" If it hurts like hell, I'll tell you not to hang the washing out; otherwise, you can count on a pretty good day. Think of it—I could put every weatherman out of business and we'd all be the better for it. Well, it's just a theory.

I shrugged on the embroidered terry-cloth robe, which was one of the last things my former wife, Lydia, gave me, the others being an occasional facial tic and a lifelong hatred of divorce lawyers. The robe always makes me feel as if I'm on my way to the Golden Gloves, but it's warm and I've gotten used to it. The broken-down Topsider moccasins were in their usual place by the front door. Easing into them, I wandered out to pick up this morning's disaster ration, as provided by the *Fort Lauderdale News & Sun Sentinel*. It's really a pretty good newspaper, but, circulation people being what they are, horror always outsells good news; the people at the *News & Sun Sentinel* were not about to flaunt that rule of journalism.

I can't face the morning paper without nourishment, so I set the paper on the sideboard and went pottering into what a former lady of residence used to call "the gallery"—a term that always unnerved Ollie Morse. Some homegrown orange juice, a couple of Mr. Thomas's English muffins, and coffee should just about do it, I thought, with a little of that super English marmalade contributed to the larder one weekend by a smashing young thing from BOAC. Pamela, my luv, I don't know whether your marmalade or your ability to keep the top up on that incredible bathing suit is the major engineering feat—both are heroic examples of human achievement.

Okay, Cam, my boy, here's the deal, I thought to myself, breakfast, then the paper, then call off the fishing trip, then figure what to do with the rest of this singularly unpromising day.

The paper warned me in no uncertain terms that I had only four more shopping days until Christmas. Since I'm no longer in the Christmas shopping business, I decided this year's Noel efforts would consist of sending the alimony check to Lydia *before* the lawyer called. Probably send them *both* into shock.

The choice of the day's activities seemed to boil down to either replacing the washers on the faucets in the guest-room shower or fixing a feedback squeal that had recently developed in the left-hand Bose stereo speaker. Neither exactly mind-bending projects, but certainly suited to a slow, gray day.

In the midst of this gloomy thought, the kitchen telephone rang. When the phone was installed, a hard-sell telephone company representative had conned me into the superlong extension cord. At the time, I thought it was frivolous, but experience has taught me differently. Among other things, it lets me girl watch or boat watch while listening to Lydia's lawyer tell me what a terrible person I am and what unspeakable indignities he has planned for me. It also lets me sit in comfort in the breakfast booth, which I did, tucking the receiver under my jaw to allow free access to the hot coffee. I would have recognized that incredible basso profundo anyway, but the opening line stopped me short. "Angus," it boomed, "is that you, Angus?" My full name, testimony to a fifth-generation burst of Scottish national pride, is Angus Cameron MacCardle (number eighty-eight in your program, number one in your hearts, fans). My older brother, probably concerned about the social liability of having a brother named Angus, hung the name Cam on me, and it's been Cam ever since.

There are only two people in the world who ever call me Angus and they do it for very different reasons. One of them is Lydia, who does it to annoy me—which, from her, it does. The other is my best friend, the Right Reverend Gerald R. Graham, pastor of Saint Paul's Church in Boca Raton— known to all, for obvious reasons, as "Billy." And he only does it to put me off balance, or when he needs help, which is infrequently, so I paid close attention.

"Angus, listen up. I've got real trouble on my hands."

"Hey, whatever happened to the *good* old words like 'Hello,' 'How've you been?' 'How about a beer?' all those terrific things?"

"You're not hearing me, Angus. I'm trying to tell you I've got one I just don't know how to deal with."

"How bad could it be? A slowdown in the Mission Fund, somebody got his hand in the poor box? What's so big you can't handle?"

"A little more serious, old friend. The lawyer thinks the district attorney will try for Murder One."

For a moment it didn't sink in, until I realized the pain in my hand came from its clamp on the receiver.

"What? Murder One? You? I can't believe . . ."

For the first time in our conversation some of the tension went out of his voice.

"Stop babbling, you greasy-fingered has-been, it's not me. It's one of my parishioners, a man named Ralph Morgan. A week ago his wife was murdered. Right now he's the prime and only suspect, you read me?"

"I got it. That's as close as I've come to a heart attack since that wonderful morning in 'Nam. I'll be glad to help in any way—you know that—but, what can *I* do?"

"Be our sounding board, Cam. The lawyer and I have been working on this the whole week and we've come up empty. Maybe we're just too close to it. The lawyer's with me now. You know him, it's Dick Ellis. He was with us on that bone fishing trip to Marathon last March with the Boys Club."

I *did* know Dick Ellis. He was a great fishing partner, easygoing, affable, pulling his share of the little unpleasant tasks, making sure all the boys got equal fishing time. A good guy without being goody-goody about it. The boys had liked him instantly—which is almost always a sure sign. I had also read, because Dick would never mention it, that he was a brilliant trial lawyer, with a ten-year record of major successes achieved from the time he graduated from Stetson. The Ellis family had been in Florida almost as long as the Seminole and there was already some talk in Tallahassee about a political career for Dick. All in all, a very good man to have on your side.

"I remember him. Why don't you fold him into that most unreverendlike van of yours and bring him over here? With that kind of talent you shouldn't stay empty very long."

"We'll be there in about half an hour, but you better know one thing before we start. Dick thinks this one is hopeless."

I said good-bye, hung up the phone, and got another cup of coffee to think by. As far as I knew, Dick Ellis was the best legal mind available in this neck of the woods. Given his track record, how could anything be hopeless? On the other hand, if he thought it was, what good would it do for me, of all people, to play sounding board?

I finally decided that we might as well turn over the cards and see what was on the table. Besides, I thought, you *owe* Billy one, and he did ask for help, Angus or no Angus.

So, I started cleaning up the breakfast stuff and put on another pot of coffee. As I worked, my mind flashed back to the first time I ever met the Right Reverend Graham.

And I smiled.

And shook my head.

3

Gerry Graham—of course he wasn't called Billy in those days—was probably the worst recruit in the history of the United States Marine Corps. He was a tough little kid out of South Philadelphia who came to Parris Island literally one step ahead of the law. A compassionate juvenile court judge had given him the choice: three years in reform school or three years in the Marine Corps. Lenient recruiting standards took care of the rest.

And he tried—Lord God, how he tried. But somehow the world had dealt him a short ration of good luck and good timing. It was always Graham who was out of step in close-order drills, Graham who fell asleep in M-16 weaponry class, Graham who dropped his rifle and had to sleep with it. Graham, Graham, Graham.

Of course the drill instructors, never one of nature's gentler breeds, came down on him like a hammer—and on me too, as his squad leader. It was either, "MacCardle, you big stupid lummox, you're responsible for that turkey. If you don't get that turd squared away in a hurry, you're gonna be a private for the rest of your miserable life." Or, "Graham, you are unquestionably the biggest shitbird of all time. If you get through boot camp—which I seriously doubt—I'm going to ship you so far away the CIA won't be able to find you." Or even worse, "Girls [all drill instructors' favorite epithet], you're probably wondering why you're standing in the rain while everybody else in this goddamned camp is eating. We're gonna *stay* out here until that silly son of a bitch Graham learns how to execute a right-flank march. Doesn't that make you tingle all over, girls? It doesn't? Well, whatcha gonna do about it?"

It finally got so bad that Graham came to me one night to tell me he couldn't take it anymore, that he was going over the hill. I really felt sorry for him—I knew what he'd been through and how much he wanted to make it in the "straight" world. So I told him, "Graham, you haven't got the system figured out yet. There have been thousands of people just like us who have gone through this thing; there's going to be thousands more after us. These guys don't know who you are. They don't know the real Gerry Graham and they don't really give a good goddamn. To them you're just a number, a piece of goods, something to cut, shape, and fit into what they call a Marine. So just relax, kid. Concentrate on what you're doing, don't let the bastards get to you. Just remember there's a lot of other idiots in the same boat we are. If they can do it, we can do it. You got it, Graham?"

Evidently, he did. At least he got enough of it so he didn't go over the hill. And he did get better. Not great, but at least enough to get out from under the drill instructors and to graduate from boot camp with the rest of us.

On the train going west to Camp Pendleton for Advanced Infantry training, we split a bottle of Old Crow and he said, "MacCardle, I owe you a Big One. If it hadn't been for you I'd a gone over the hill—probably be in the jug back in Philly right now. I don't know how to repay you, but I'm sure as hell gonna give it a try."

I promptly forgot about it, figuring most of it had come from the Crow, and besides, I hadn't done all that much anyway. After all, talk's cheap; the system hadn't been that hard to dope out.

After Parris Island, Camp Pendleton was easy, at least from the mental harassment side. The instructors knew we were bound for Vietnam, so they concentrated on getting us ready to go to war and with any kind of luck to come out the other side. We got a lot more experience with all sorts of weaponry, hand-to-hand combat techniques, and some delightful little tricks I don't even like to remember.

They also ran us up and down every hill on the base, and believe me, Camp Pendleton has a bunch of hills. We never could figure what lugging forty pounds up and down a hill had to do with jungle warfare, but if the Marine Corps wanted us to climb hills, we'd climb hills. When the time came to go to 'Nam we were ready—at least physically.

I don't talk much about Vietnam. I never have and I never will. The heat, the rain, the bugs, and the constant fear were *our* Vietnam—all best forgotten if you can do it. There weren't any winners. Only losers, lots and lots of losers. Civilians and combatants. The dead, the wounded, and the crazies. All losers. The most tragic were the guys who made it through okay and came home to find America was ashamed of them, had turned its back on them, didn't want anything to do with the war or the guys who were sent to fight it. We're still trying to straighten that one out, but we've got a long way to go. A lousy deal all around.

The two things I do remember clearly happened on the same day, a little short of a year after we'd gotten to 'Nam. Graham and I were still together, which is unusual, but it does happen—the Marine Corps is a pretty small outfit.

We'd gone out on a night patrol and gotten cut off, pinned down by enemy fire. We dug into the bush as much as we could. Sometime in the night, Gerry took a bullet in the shoulder. In the morning we found out it was really smashed. All I could do was sprinkle some of the sulfa powder on it and strap on a field bandage.

To make things worse, the dengue fever I'd been fighting for over six months kicked up again. So we stayed hidden, listening to the fighting ebb and flow all around, Gerry nursing his shoulder, me getting hotter and dizzier from the fever.

During the night, Gerry whispered, "If we get out of this thing, I'm going to give my life to God. I'm gonna become a minister. I swear to God."

I didn't think much of it at the time. Such promises were pretty commonplace in Vietnam, probably have been all the way back to the Roman legion—"Jupiter, spare me from the Gauls and I'll sacrifice a lamb every week." Lots of promises—some of which actually got kept.

At dawn, a bunch of those big Huey gunships came up from behind and just blew away the jungle up ahead of us. We figured nothing could have lived through that fire storm, so we dug out and started back in the direction the Hueys had come from.

We couldn't make very good time—I was half carrying Gerry and fighting not to pass out. The drill was, go a couple hundred meters and rest, then repeat the process. Slow and steady. It almost got us killed.

We pulled off the trail and I'd just taken off my helmet when I heard a dull thud. I looked down at the ground and saw it—a genuine, U.S. regulation, fragmentation grenade. Three-second fuse, big bang, lots of deadly parts. I thought to myself, Cam, that's it—that's the ball game.

Gerry never hesitated. With a lurch, he dove past me, torn shoulder and all, onto the grenade. It went off right on schedule—with a nice, light pop. Some careless, overpaid munitions worker had bungled the job. Let's hear it for inefficiency.

But Gerry hadn't known that. There was a job to be done and he did it—simple as that. I was crying when I picked him up, crying when I slung him over my shoulder, crying when we stumbled into our own lines.

Macho Marines never cry, right? Forget about it.

They sent us down to Saigon, me to get the dengue under control, Gerry to get a patch-together of the shoulder and then shipment home, where they could get the big job done.

Just before he left, they wheeled him into my ward and we visited for a while, promising we'd get together when it was over, promising to telephone and write regularly—all those good things. None of which happened, at least not for a long time.

*   *   *

The final score was 49–14—a game best forgotten quickly. I was so tired I thought, They're just gonna have to *cut* the uniform off me. They can start with the cleats, then the trou, then the cup, then the pads, right on up to the hat— the whole nine yards.

It was midway through my second year with the Big Blue, a rebuilding year according to the papers. A few more games like this, methought, and they can start rebuilding *me*.

The Steelers had come to town and just destroyed us. What a score—there must have been a lot of happy bookies in Pittsburgh that afternoon. The defense they called the Steel Curtain controlled the line of scrimmage, shut down our running game, and forced my Main Man to put the ball up forty-four times.

The only happy thought was, since we were in different conferences, the schedule said we wouldn't play Pittsburgh again for another five years. There *is* a wideness in God's mercy.

I finally got the gear off and struggled into the shower. Another big mistake. The hit signs were already beginning to show where the linebackers had gotten their piece on the underpatterns, where the DBs had gotten to me on the curls and flags. Tomorrow, the newspaper headlines would say MAC-CARDLE CATCHES 7. My *body's* headline would be SEND ME TO THE MAYO CLINIC.

I trudged back to my locker and slumped onto the little stool thinking, You can do it, boy. First the clothes, then the cab, then the apartment, then collapse. C'mon, champ, one task at a time.

One of the clubhouse attendants tapped me on the shoulder. My first thought was that somebody from the media wanted to talk to me. I couldn't imagine why, but then the ghoul rate in the press was running high that year. Ah, well, we'll just get it over with; they gotta make a living too.

That wasn't the message, though. The attendant said, "There's a priest or a reverend or somethin' outside wants to

speak to you, Mr. MacCardle. Said his name was Graham.
But he didn't call you Cam like everybody else, said to ask
Angus if he could come in. Want me to get rid of him for
you?"

Angus? Angus? It had to be Gerry Graham, and it was,
all five feet six of him with that voice that sounded like the
PA system at the stadium. And, by God, he was a "priest or a
reverend or somethin'" too, with the turned-around collar to
prove it.

We shook and hugged and thumped on each other like
boys. I told him if he would go get us a cab, I'd spring for
dinner—we could play catch-up. I was so pleased to see him
again, the tiredness and the pain melted away. I threw on my
clothes, including the ratty old tie I retrieved from the back of
the locker, said good night to the survivors, walked out, and
jumped into Gerry's cab.

"Christ Cella," I said to the driver, "Forty-sixth between
Third and Lex."

"Wuddiya think I am, from outta town? I know where
Christ Cella is, Mac," he snarled. New York cabdrivers—
truly a breed apart.

Christ Cella is my absolute all-time favorite restaurant.
Courtesy of the NFL schedule makers, I'd sampled some
good ones—Loch Ober, The Blue Fox, Chateaubriande, Gal-
lotoire's, and so on—but if I had one meal left in the world,
I'd pick Christ Cella's. During Prohibition it was a speakeasy.
It still holds some of that flavor—sawdust on the floor, plain
white tablecloths, army-issue cutlery, and waiters with aprons.
It's hard to get a table, particularly without a reservation, but
John, the maitre d', and I had become pretty good friends; he
always tucked me away where only the waiters could find me.
The service is quick and the food is superb—what's supposed
to be hot is hot and vice versa—served in portions that would
stun your average lion. If you're a lamb chop freak—which I
am—Christ Cella has the finest lamb chops in the world, truly
the Sistine Chapel of lamb chops.

We walked in, I introduced Gerry to John, and he did his

number, finding room for us in the back of the kitchen, which, believe it or not, is the best seat in the house. As further proof of our friendship, John didn't mention the game, though I knew he was a big fan, and he'd surely been there. Good man, John.

We ordered, the drinks came, and we went through the usual toasting process: to us, the bad old times, to the good times, to those who made it and those who didn't. Then the lamb chops, as big and juicy as I'd promised, with hash browns, a super blue cheese dressing, and a bottle of Beaujolais.

Finally came the time for brandy, cigars, and talk. I opened:

"You did it, Gerry, by . . . gosh, you really did it. You said you would and you did, now tell me how, your worship."

"You first, gracious host," he rumbled.

So I did, trying to keep it as short as possible, since nothing in the world is as boring to me as hearing me talk about me.

"By the time they got the dengue fever under control, my tour was up and they shipped me back to Camp Lejeune to a Special Services unit. I spent the rest of my hitch keeping America safe from communism by passing out socks and jocks to the troops. I got out, went back to Penn State, majored in history. An assistant coach saw me playing in a fraternity-league basketball game and told Joe Paterno about me. I really didn't want to play football, figuring the books and the laundry concession and a lady or two were a plateful, but Mr. Paterno is a very convincing person. One thing I felt good about, Gerry, was that Mr. Paterno insisted all of his players get their degrees. I didn't realize how unusual that was until I started swapping stories at training camp. Some guy, Mr. Paterno. He would have made a helluva Marine. Anyway, I played for him my junior and senior years; we did pretty well and I got drafted in the third round. So here I am, a bona fide college graduate making a living playing a boy's game. How's that for instant history?"

"Not bad," he said, smiling. "You only left out the all-American mentions and that incredible catch in the Sugar Bowl. You've become a modest soul in your dotage, Angus. I'm not sure it becomes you. How about another glass of brandy to dull the senses, or have you spent all the signing bonus money?" We ordered and he went on.

"Mine's a little different and not nearly as glamorous. The shoulder was worse than even we figured it and they finally sent me to Bethesda, where the biggies could work on it. The whole thing took a little more than a year and they got it back to about fifty percent. I think I am the only Episcopal priest who consecrates the bread and the cup one-handed. It used to startle the bishop, but I think he's used to it now. Anyway, I knew I couldn't keep my promise without higher education and I did have all that time staring me in the face.

"One of the nurse friendlies had a brother who was a senior in high school in D.C., so I got her to bring me a copy of each one of his textbooks. I read them all, backward and forward, cover to cover, including the little tests at the ends of the chapters. I must have been some sight, arm up in the air, that huge cast with the weights hanging off, trying to juggle a ruler, a protractor, and a geometry book. It's a wonder no one got hurt.

"Then I got some good news and bad news all the same day. The bad news was the doctors had to do another operation, which was going to chew up three more months. The good news I got from the Navy Personnel guy in charge of my case. He told me the Navy had a high school equivalancy exam that they use to screen enlisted candidates for the NAV-CAD aviation program and for Annapolis. Colleges accept it the same as a high school diploma. He got it for me, I took it and sent it in, and two months later, I got this little certificate. It's no big deal, but I felt like I'd just graduated from Harvard.

"Meanwhile, one of the surgeons was after me to go to his school, in Tennessee. People call it Sewanee, but its real name is the University of the South. It's a liberal arts school, but they also have an Episcopal seminary there; you can combine credits if you want to get through as quickly as possible, which was just what I wanted. The surgeon wrote them a letter and it must have worked, because they wrote back and accepted me whenever I could start.

"By then, the doctors were done with me and so was the Marine Corps. I got my discharge, bought some civilian clothes, and got on the bus for Sewanee. You know, Cam, after Parris Island I swore I'd never set foot in the South again, and there I was going right back. Pretty weird.

"I didn't have much money—the G.I. Bill and my combat pay and the disability checks only go so far—and I wanted to make up for lost time. A scholarship the last two years helped put it over the top. The living was okay—I waited tables nights and weekends, got my room and board from one of the fraternity houses for sweeping up and tending the furnace and grounds. There were times when things got tight, but I had The Promise to keep, and somehow it all worked itself out.

"I finished Sewanee and got really lucky, doing my curacy at a big church in Atlanta that had the reputation of being a boot camp for young ministers. Got ordained there and later was contacted by a member of the Search Committee from Saint Paul's in Boca Raton. They interviewed me, guess they liked what they heard, and that's where I went. I was delighted, because I've come to love the South. I don't exactly know why—the years in Tennessee, the time in Georgia, the climate, the people, the traditions, just what—but I knew I wanted to stay south. So here I am, a busted-up ex-Marine, with a funny collar, ministering to the Blue-Haired Brigade in South Florida. Not nearly as exciting as your life, Cam, but I did keep The Promise."

No, I thought, exciting doesn't really cover it. An educational system dropout and potential reform school inmate, in agony between operations, teaches himself high school in a hospital bed. Then crams college and seminary together on no money, earns a scholarship, and winds up with a post in an established church. It made me feel like a spoiled, over-privileged jock, which I was. It also made me awfully proud of Gerry.

Of course I didn't say that. I just reached over, clinked glasses, and said, as evenly as I could, "You did fine, Peerless Prelate, you did just fine."

The telephone rang, cutting across my train of thought, shaking me out of memory's depths like an ice-cold shower.

You're getting to be an old dog, MacCardle, I thought, lying in the sun and dreaming about the past. Up boy, good dog, steady fella.

"Cam, Dick Ellis here. I know we said we'd be right by, but I just got reminded I've got a court appearance at eleven. Thank God for beepers and smart secretaries or I'd probably forget my trousers. The court thing is no big deal, but I have to be there. Shouldn't take more than hour, hour and a half at most. Billy will pick me up, we'll get some sandwiches and come by your place around one—okay with you?"

"Sure, Counselor, be good to see you again, even granted the circumstances. Tell him to go to the Italian deli on Sample Road—he knows where it is. Anything you want'll be superb. Please tell Mario I said that, ask him for some of his special Dijon mustard on my ham and provolone. I've got chips and drinkables right here, so don't bother about that. One o'clock's fine with me. Say, Richard, can you give me any better feeling for what this is all about?"

"Can't, Cam. I gotta run and this deal takes time to explain. I'll tell you one thing, though, if I—we—can get this guy off, it'll make Clarence Darrow look like a first-year law student."

"That good, huh, Counselor?"

"That bad. We'll see you around one."

So, one o'clock it would have to be. Must be a dandy if Dick Ellis, Mr. Unflappable, was talking that way.

I went back to the mindless chores of the morning—finished up the breakfast stuff, dumped a load of laundry into

the washer, shaved, showered, got dressed. Ran the Elec-
trolux around for a while, got another cup of coffee, flipped
on the tube, and sank back into the six-cushioned couch that
somebody had christened the U.S.S. *Lexington*. Cam Mac-
Cardle, all-American housewife.

Merv Griffin was interviewing an improbable-looking English matron, all jaw and tweed, about her latest book, which
evidently demonstrated that a daily massage for your dog did
wonders for pet and owner alike. Merv is the very best of the
talk-show hosts, but even he couldn't rise above that kind of
material, and my mind wandered away, back to remembering
about Billy and how much his friendship had meant to me
over the years.

After the reunion dinner, we did a much better job of
staying in touch, mostly thanks to Gerry. About once a month
I could count on a long, wryly amusing letter from him, full of
news about his job, the parishioners, and South Florida in
general. He'd learned the fine art of not taking himself over-
seriously—much of the humor coming at his own expense.

One of his early letters had a story that really tickled me
and I read it aloud to the troops. Apparently, one of his GPs
(Grateful Parishioners, a term I think he swiped from the
medics) had invited Gerry to his country club for a Sunday
afternoon swim. At some point he'd spotted an extremely attractive young lady, and being a red-blooded American male,
he'd walked over and introduced himself. They'd spent the
rest of the afternoon together, splashing around the pool,
talking about a million things, ending the day with a drink at
the outdoor bar. About that time, Gerry decided his evening
would be improved considerably if he took her out to dinner,
so he asked her and was delighted when it turned out she was
free. They agreed to meet back at the bar and went into the
locker rooms to change. Evidently she was a quicker dresser
than he—she was at the bar when he came out. He spotted
her, walked over, tapped her on the shoulder. She turned,
recognized him . . . and fainted. Seems their conversation had

covered just about everything *but* what Gerry did for a living; the sight of him in his summer weights, with the collar and all, just put her away. He said it took him two weeks to convince her that in his religion, the occasional drink, dating, and even marriage were all legit. Their relationship never got off the ground. Even though he wore civilian clothes when he took her out, every time he tried to kiss her, she'd simply freeze. Finally he asked her what the problem was, and she'd said, in a little squeak, "Gerry, I'd love to, but I feel like God's watching."

The guys loved the story, and her words became our unofficial motto for the balance of the miserable season. The funniest example happened in our second Dallas game, the season closer. It was late in the fourth quarter; as usual, we were losing big. One of their blitzing linebackers got by our center, Bob Bucciarelli, and just leveled the Main Man. After scraping himself off the deck he grabbed Butch, told him to *hold* the linebacker, if that's what it took. Butch looked down at him and said in a falsetto, "I'll try it, Main Man, if you're sure God ain't watching!" I was laughing so hard I didn't want to leave the huddle.

Gerry's letters became a part of all of our lives. If we hadn't heard from him in a while, the troops would come around to make sure he was all right. Bucciarelli said it best: "We gotta keep in touch with him, Cam. We're the only team in the NFL with a captive reverend, and God knows we need all the help we can get."

I kept up my end mostly by relying on Ma Bell. For some reason, which I'm sure the squirrel doctors could explain in depth, I'm a terrible correspondent. I love to get letters, but writing, to me, is a torture. Lydia used to say my letters reminded her of the obligatory Sunday letters young campers write home each week in trade for supper—no letter, no supper. "Dear Folks, I'm O.K. How are you and how is Rags? Well, that's all for now. Your son, Herbie."

When my mother died, Dad and I went through the sad process of sorting her personal effects. I was touched to discover that she had saved all of my letters, more than some-what chagrined to find out there was a grand total of nine. I really loved you, Ma; I just wasn't very good at putting it on paper.

In one of the phone calls, Gerry invited me to come spend a couple of weeks with him in mid-May—which I did—and I enjoyed myself so much that it became an annual pil-grimage. South Florida in May is an absolute delight. The weather is generally clear and warm, without the skull-busting heat that July and August bring. The Canadians and the snowbirds are gone, most of the good restaurants and major attractions are still open, and the prices come down to near-affordable levels.

Tourism is to South Florida, as the poet Kris Kristoffer-son wrote, "a blessing and a curse." Florida treats her visitors well and so she should: tourism is the largest single compo-nent of the gross state product. It is also the cleanest form of revenue there is. The tourists come, spend wads of money, and depart. No need for extra schools, sewage facilities, po-lice, fire fighters, or other civil servants. Truly a renewable financial feast.

The fiscal bonanza brings problems as well. The highways become almost impassable, the beaches are overcrowded, and unless you can adjust to eating supper at four or ten-thirty, you can forget your favorite restaurant from December through April. Veteran Floridians have developed a survival formula for the Season: stock up the larder, batten down the hatches, and bless the cable television system that brings in everything but the BBC.

I used the two weeks principally as a pre-training-camp revitalization process—a chance to regain lost muscle tone and shed some of the evils the off-season wreaks on the body. I didn't go to as many banquets as the Main Man, but I got my share of them. The Rubber Chicken and the Bonhomie circuits may do wonders for public relations and season ticket sales, but for the ballplayer, it puts a burden on the body that no amount of swimming, squash, or indoor exercise can compensate for, certainly not in my case.

So, the Florida pilgrimmage became part of my personal rites of spring—part pleasure, part business. A chance to catch up socially with Gerry and his growing group of friends, a chance for the body to gain benefit from an informal program of running, surf swimming, and the ultimate test—volleyball games in the sand, man's greatest inhumanity to man. All things told, an enjoyable, rewarding time, much anticipated during the raw bleakness of a New York City winter.

In my third season we played the Dolphins in the Orange Bowl, which finally gave the troops a chance to meet the captive reverend in person. Though we'd done some planning for the occasion, the results exceeded even our expectations.

Gerry brought a bunch of kids from a settlement house to one of our practice sessions and it was a real toss-up as to who had the better time. The kids, fueled by a seemingly endless supply of hot dogs and Cokes, enjoyed every fan's dream of being able to meet a whole group of major-league ballplayers—as Mr. Cosell puts it—"up close and personal." The troops loved it too, seeing it not as a media event but as a chance to help some kids to whom life hadn't been overly kind. On the other side, some semi-obscure athletes found themselves surrounded by youngsters who *really* wanted to know who they were and what they were about—a most rewarding experience all around.

That night, Gerry brought the first of a series of his improbable vans around to the hotel, and we piled into it to go to supper—Gerry and I, the Main Man, Butch and Hammerin' Henry Munroe, one of our DBs. Henry always told the media he was the token black man in our crowd, but it wasn't true. Henry was our token *defensive* player—on a team that, at least that year, saw a minimum of civility between the two squads.

We went to Bobby Rubino's Restaurant—The Place for Ribs—now justly famous for serving mountains of ribs with a supersecret sauce and loaves of onion rings, which guaranteed the eater a cool reception in the huddle the next day, if not longer. Bucciarelli led the league by putting away four helpings of everything—the last provided on the house by a somewhat startled management—and even Henry, pride of Mobile and Grambling University, connoisseur supreme of barbeque, allowed they were the best he'd ever had. Mr. Rubino, may you continue to grow and flourish as one of the last of the honest restauranteurs in a world where nobody seems to give a damn anymore about providing service, quality, and value for the money.

What was the final score of the game? That was the season the Dolphins put it all together, hanging up that probably unreachable 17–0 record, ending with an overwhelming display in the Super Bowl. Kiick and the Big Zonk, Griese, Twilley and Warfield, the No-Name Defense. It was the only unpleasant experience in an otherwise memorable week.

The next year, Lydia came into my life. Lydia Longstreet Vance, fairest of the fair, The Belle of Charlotte, The Pearl of the Piedmont. A Miss America face, a chorus girl's body, and an inquisitive mind that even four years of Sweet Briar couldn't dull—a most impressive package by anybody's standards. I met her at one of those interminable East Village cocktail parties where far too many people are crammed into an apartment to drink warm wine, breathe in the used marijuana smoke, and roar at one another to prove who's most with it. I'd made the mistake of refereeing an argument between a decidedly delicate chap and a hairy-legged Hunter College horror on whether Mary Cassatt had been influenced more by Degas or Manet. Not exactly a cosmic topic, but then I was pretty bored. All-out war was shaping up between my two combatants, when I suddenly felt an insistent tugging at my elbow. I turned just enough to catch sight of a startlingly pretty girl, making gestures for me to bend over so she could be heard over the din. Which I promptly did—only to hear a marvelously round, soft voice say, "Darlin', we'd best get you out of here before one or the other of 'em takes a notion to scratch your eyes out."

We went to Peter's Backyard, where we had a couple of big steaks plus a good little Bordeaux and the first of what Lydia called "them ramblin' lil' chats." We rambled all right, up to the point where the boss came by and asked if we wouldn't like to come back some other time, since the waiters had all gone home and it was coming up on one-thirty in the morning.

During the "ramblin'" she discovered that all athletes aren't necessarily confined to a knowledge of Xs and Os. For my part, I found she'd taken the glorious Lydia package, added a Columbia MBA to it, and was up to her pretty little ears in the Personal Trust Division of Citibank, dealing with annuities, money market funds, tax-free municipals, and other mind-numbing instruments.

We started dating, infrequently at first, then more regularly, and finally exclusively—to the point where I asked her to marry me and she accepted, though not without the mandatory trips to Charlotte and Philadelphia for the parental blessings of the banns.

I guess I did all right in Charlotte, or as well as could be expected, but the Philadelphia chapter turned into a rout. My father, the doctor, who approved neither of what I did for a living nor of my previous taste in female companions, was predisposed to dismiss her as "another of Cam's bits of fluff." Well, Lydia turned on the afterburners and just charmed him right out of his socks. Final score: Potential Father-in-Law 0, Lydia 35 and pulling away at the gun.

Of course, I wanted Gerry to perform the ceremony and, of course, that just wouldn't do at all. "Cam, honey, Mama and Big Lydia and Daddy wouldn't understand, poor Mr. Hostetter would simply die." Even then I should have known.

Anyway, poor Mr. Hostetter married us and Gerry was best man—in civilian clothes, of course, "to avoid confusion." The week before the wedding was a blur of activity, ending with a stag dinner that had all the grace and charm of a medieval boar hunt. Finally, just to put some points on the board, Gerry proposed a toast to the groom. By then it was a matter of too little, too late.

Somehow Lydia held the whole thing together—through and including a wedding reception that must have cost Daddy at least five years' worth of "Coke-Cola dividends."

Then Gerry drove us to the airport, blessed the marriage one more time, and put us on the plane to Antigua—number one on Lydia's limited list of non-tacky places—and a lifetime of happiness.

At least, that's what we thought at the time.

I heard the crunch of gravel as Billy's van pulled into my driveway and got up to let them in.

4

The rain hit just as I swung the door open, that pelting, drenching rain the locals call a "frawg strangler." Shortly, the streets would be awash, the storm drains overflowing, the motorists inching cautiously through miniature lakes that had been dry pavement only minutes before. Then, just as quickly as they had come, the heavy black-gray clouds would scud ponderously out to sea, like so many ancient Spanish galleons, dumping the balance of their cargoes where it wouldn't do anybody any good. The sun would reappear, making short work of the instant lakes and causing sheets of steam to rise from the streets as it completed the drying-out cycle. Meanwhile, the frawgs were in for a tough time.

They came scuttling in, Billy bent over nearly double to protect the big bag of sandwiches from the rain. I took the sandwiches and left the two of them squelshing around noisily in my tiled foyer while I went to fetch two big terry-cloth towels from the poolroom locker. The toweling process restored them to a recognizable form of humanity, except for Dick's seersucker suit, which looked as if he'd been swimming in it.

In my house, nobody wears shoes. It's a custom I picked up in the pre-Lydia days in New York when I was dating a Japanese interpreter from the UN. It is one of Japan's great contributions to mankind. Aside from the practical value— principally less wear and tear on floors and rugs— "no shoes" has the amazing ability to reduce people's stuffiness quotient.

It's very difficult to pontificate when you look down at your feet and see dragons staring back at you. So I have a huge shoe tree in the foyer for people to hang their conventional footwear on and a mound of various-size scuffs, most of which actually match. Now semi-dry and properly shod, I brought Dick and Billy into the living room, installed them on the *Lexington*, gave both of them a beer, and left them to chat while I went back to the galley to unpack the groceries and lay out luncheon gear.

True to form, the clouds were disappearing and I could see patches of sunlight glinting off the surface of the canal. Might as well eat and talk on the dock, I thought; it sure beats the hell out of sitting around in the air conditioning. The dock is eighty feet long and it's one of the major reasons why I bought the house. It will accommodate the boats of anybody I care to know. At the far end I'd installed a wet bar, with an awning and some all-weather, low-back barstools. I stacked the luncheon makings on a tray, scooped up Billy and Dick, dried off the stool seats, and laid out the lunch on the bar.

Interrupting my concentration on one of Mario's better ham and provolone efforts, Dick Ellis said, "You know, Cam, I've never been here before. I really like it—house, dock, the oversize pool, *and* the location. You did right well for a new-comer."

Actually, I hadn't found it at all; one of Billy's Blue-Haired Brigade had. She had a niece who was a realtor in Boca Raton, and once I'd decided to live in South Florida, Billy sicced the both of them on me. Talk about aggressive— the niece could have given Bucciarelli cards and spades and still beaten him to death. For two solid weeks I was poked and pried and chivied all over Broward and Palm Beach counties. I have a feeling about realtors. I think if you told them your absolute tops was five million dollars, they'd say, "Oh, dear, if you could only come up with five million five, I could really show you something just right." The pitch never changes, only the money.

Anyway, in our searching I found myself drawn again

and again to Lighthouse Point. It's a little village between Federal Highway and the Intracoastal Waterway, hidden between the sprawls of Pompano Beach and Deerfield Beach. There was something comfortable about it, a laid-back community of well-tended houses and pleasant-looking people. The residents turned out to be a mixture of retireds, doctors, and airline captains, of sufficient age so that I needn't worry about tons of little kiddies or the motorcycle crowd. The niece sealed it for me when she said, "Well, of course, it isn't Boca Raton. But [sigh] if that's what you want, that's where we'll concentrate." So we did. Three weeks later I bought the house from an Eastern Airlines captain and his second wife, who were being transferred to New York. They'd done a wonderful job with it, enclosing the former patio and transforming it into a sort of great room that ran the length of the house, with a far wall that was mostly sliding glass windows that looked out onto the screened-in pool, the expanse of the dock, and the canal.

It's two canals away from the Intracoastal and a five-minute shot to the ocean through the Hillsboro Inlet, which is so safe that even I could navigate it without running anyone else aground. Shortly after I bought the house, I got conned into acquiring a slightly elderly but most seaworthy thirty-six-foot Hatteras cruiser from an old gaffer in Vero Beach who didn't want to deal anymore with the effort and expense to keep her up. She was just the right size for me, small enough so as not to overwhelm my lack of experience, big enough for off-shore fishing and, if I got really brave, a run to the Keys or over to Nassau. For some inexplicable reason she'd been named the *Gull-O-Teen* when I bought her and I knew *that* would never do. A group of us spent a hilarious Saturday in a naming bee, the candidates becoming increasingly bawdy as the night progressed and grape flowed. I finally named her *Smollert's Folly*, living proof that The Pearl's blackhearted lawyer hadn't yet reduced my standard of living to the poverty level, though, heaven knows, he had done his best.

We sat at the bar, drinking beer and chewing up Mario's

handiwork, the only other noise coming from the *Folly's* automatic bilge pumps as they disposed of the last of the rain.

Finished, I pushed my stool back and looked over at them. "Okay, guys, not that this isn't all very pleasant, but would you mind telling me what's going on?"

"You go first, Dick," Billy said, "you've been more involved with the police investigation part of it. Fire away."

Ellis sat, not moving a muscle, obviously trying to put his thoughts together. Finally he said, "Cam, I'm not being coy, I'm just trying to figure out the best way to lay it out. Let me start by telling you how I got involved and we'll just go on from there. As Billy told you this morning, the guy's name is Morgan, Ralph Morgan. His wife's name is—or was—Laura Morgan, Laura Evans Morgan, to be precise. He's a stockbroker with one of those huge New York outfits, works out of a branch office in a big industrial complex on Oakland Park Boulevard, down in Lauderdale. Fairly near our place. I don't know him very well—I met him a couple of times at Rotary Club luncheons, saw him occasionally at Chamber functions. He's not an easy man to know, either; I wonder how he makes a living in the stock market business. Most of those guys are the typical professional salesmen, all teeth, a firm handshake, the look-'em-in-the-eye sincere sell. Not Ralph Morgan.

"He's more like what the British science community calls a back-office boffin, people who are great at the technical side of things but are also generally regarded as unfit for public consumption. Not that Ralph is obnoxious—quite the opposite. I guess the word for him is 'reserved.' A dime-store psychologist would probably refer to him as introverted. Whatever, the man treats words like emeralds; you have to drag conversation out of him. What eventually emerges is worthwhile, he can even be amusing, but the conversational process is a true job of work. He seems bright, too, but if I were running that show, I think I'd use Ralph for all the inside work and get me a crew of real hustlers to do the selling.

"As far as Laura Morgan goes, the late Laura Morgan I should say, she's a total blank to me—never met her.

"Anyway, there's a young man in our firm named Tom Horton—don't think either of you know him—he's one of Judge Harlan Horton's boys and the judge and my father go back to the year one. Tom got his law degree from the University of Virginia about four years back and Dad asked me if I would interview him. Well, I hate that kind of political goings-on, but I interviewed the boy, liked him very much, hired him, and he's been with us ever since—doing very well, I might add."

I was beginning to wonder where all this was heading, if we'd *ever* get to the point. Lydia was like that, starting a sentence that then developed several subpoints, which in turn spawned other sidetracks, until I forgot what she had started out to say. One thing about Ellis, I thought, he wasn't going to underwhelm us with details. I realized he was still talking.

"Unbeknown to me, three, maybe three and a half years ago, Morgan called the firm, said he'd just gotten married and wanted somebody to do up a will for him and his bride. As you might imagine, that kind of assignment gets handed out to one of the juniors, so Tom Horton wound up with the job. Tom remembers them as pretty simple wills—not much cash or other tangible assets involved—there weren't and aren't any children.

"The morning after the police took Morgan in, he called Tom, sketched out the problem, and asked Tom to come see him. Tommy went over there, listened to Morgan, realized the thing was well beyond his depth, came back to the firm, and got hold of me straightaway. Tom also told me Morgan had asked him to call Billy. I said I could take care of that, seeing as we'd known each other for a while, and I did.

"Billy and I finally got to see Morgan about three that afternoon, and I must say I felt sorry for him. He looked terrible—he was probably *still* in shock—and it took even longer than usual for us to drag the story out of him. Anyway, here's what he told us. Billy, please fill in if I skip anything."

Fat chance of that, I thought, and sure enough, he was a good forty-five minutes relating it. It was long but by no means uninteresting, an increasingly fascinating and frightening story, even thirdhand. An innocent telephone call starting a chain of events culminating in the discovery of a dead wife and Ralph being held in jail—with ten thousand questions unanswered and nobody to help. As with all recountings of other people's disasters, I found myself very glad not to be in Ralph Morgan's place.

"So, after asking if there was anything we could bring him, we left Morgan and split up. Billy went back to begin taking care of the funeral arrangements and I went downstairs to check in with Lieutenant Hampton, first name Wade. He'd been the duty officer when Laura was killed and had been assigned the responsibility for the preliminary investigation. I've know Hampton for years, so it was a pretty easy meeting, or as easy as these things ever are.

"I told him our office—probably myself—would be representing Morgan, gave him my card with the office and home phone numbers, and asked him to keep in touch.

"He said he wasn't sure the case was worthy of such talent as the 'Great Ellis.' Their preliminary reaction was that Morgan was in deep trouble. Said his boys had had more than enough to say grace over *before* Mrs. Morgan's death, but they would try to get right on it. Asked me to check with him in a couple of days and told me if anything did come up meanwhile, they'd contact me.

"I met with him yesterday afternoon and I must say, I was impressed—and depressed—by what they've turned up.

"Before I get into that, you think I could beat the house out of another cold beer? This talking's getting to be thirsty work."

For all hands, I thought, but I grinned and bent down to fish a beer out of the little refrigerator in the wet bar, uncapped it, and slid it over the Formica countertop to him.

Typically, he gave it the precision pour job, which produced the kind of picture-perfect head you always see in the commercials. He took a healthy chunk, belched slightly, and went on.

"Before I tell you what Lieutenant Hampton said, you better understand who he is. Wade Hampton has fifteen solid years on the force. Started as a patrolman and worked his way up, not as quickly as some, but he made it. Not a hint of *any* wrongdoings—no brutality, no corruption, no influence peddling. He may not be very imaginative, but he's a thorough, by-the-book, superconscientious cop and a good one.

"When we met yesterday, technically he was off duty, although a man like Hampton is probably never totally off duty. He gave me his version of the case, which is reasonably close to Morgan's, and then brought me up to date on what they'd done so far.

"When an apparent murder is involved, the responding officer—in this case a Sergeant Serkin—has a couple of principal responsibilities. The first is to clear the scene of the crime, not very difficult this time, since a condominium is pretty easy to seal off. The second is to telephone his supervisor—Hampton—and the Crime Scene Squad. The squad goes in first, inspects the premises, takes photographs, measures, that kind of thing. They also log in appropriate evidence before removing it from the scene—in this case one item was the bathrobe sash. The medical examiner then does a preliminary check on the victim and arranges to have the body taken to the lab for more extensive examination. Finally, the Homicide people get a chance to go in and do their investigating.

"While all that was going on, Hampton and the two patrolmen took Ralph in and witnessed his statement—the gist of which I just gave you."

Some gist, I thought, more like a two-hundred-page Classic Comic book.

"At our meeting yesterday, he summarized what they've done since then. I'm afraid it isn't a particularly encouraging story.

"The medical examiner confirmed death by suffocation

and strangulation some time between six and nine o'clock. Whoever did it wasn't taking any chances—for sure it rules out suicide.

"The M.E. also discovered that Laura had sexual relations sometime in the afternoon of the day she was killed. That time, because of the semen aging techniques, is evidently harder to pin down, but he was reasonably sure it had occurred after twelve and before five. Hampton asked if there were any signs of rape. The M.E. told him no; it looked as if she'd been totally cooperative. I don't know how an M.E. could tell that, but I guess we'll have to take his word. Anyway, Laura's behavior isn't what's on trial. Parenthetically, Ralph doesn't know this part of it. If we can help it, I'd just as soon not tell him.

"Blood, stomach contents, and fecal analysis show no signs of drugs. Evidently she'd had a couple of drinks of some kind of alcoholic beverage—actually, more than a couple. She was over the legal limits of sobriety, but still functioning; she wasn't 'drunk-drunk.'

"Her fingernails were clean and unbroken. Usually, in cases like that, you can hope for flesh or other foreign materials under the fingernails as a result of a struggle, but not this time. Whoever did it, did a quick sure job on her.

"The detective team went over the condominium thoroughly, found no evidence of B and E, sorry—breaking and entering—no broken windows, no lock damage, no sign of the bolt being forced.

"They dusted everything for fingerprints and sent the findings to Washington. I don't hold out much hope there, either; fingerprint evidence was passé when Perry Mason was a boy and it tends to be inconclusive at best.

"They established that Ralph had come to work right on time as usual—eight-thirty. He went to lunch alone, his secretary said, told her he was going to take a sandwich to the park by the beach. Left a little after one, got back around two-fifteen. Everyone in the office was gone by five-thirty, and all confirmed that he was at his desk when they left. A neighbor,

Mrs. Hillson, saw him leaving his condominium a little after
seven. She was walking her dog. She was positive about the
time. Evidently, she always watches the 'CBS Evening News'
on Channel Four, then walks the dog, then gets back in time
to watch 'M*A*S*H.' She said she waved at Morgan but he
didn't respond.

"They checked around the complex itself and found out
something that I didn't know but Billy did. The Morgans
weren't getting along very well, to put it mildly. Another of
the neighbors said he almost called the police one night about
two weeks ago, on account of all the noise and the quality of
the vocabulary involved.

"With Ralph's permission, they did a quick riffle through
his and her financial positions. Ralph has a two-hundred-thou-
sand dollar insurance policy—a combination straight life and
convertible term—on his life and some kind of rider on her
for ten thousand.

"They have a joint NOW account at East Coast Fidelity
with a current balance of eighty-one hundred dollars and
change. Hampton's people checked out every other bank in
town and their branches, no Ralph Morgan, no Laura Morgan. Another zippo. Ralph has a margin stock investment account with his own company in his name—total value, less
what he owes, about eleven thousand dollars at today's prices.
They owned their condo unit jointly and were mortgaged up
to their ears. He'd be lucky to get five thousand dollars out of
it after paying back the bank and the developer's supplemen-
tal financing.

"All in all, looks like they were riding the financial edge;
maybe that was what some of the squabbling was about. In
any event, whoever killed Laura surely didn't do it for the
money.

"They checked out the mysterious Mr. Anderson and
that's a dead end. Anderson may or may not exist. What they
did was telephone the so-called mutual friend, a Mr. Carl
Ballantine. Ballantine turned out to be extremely cooperative, but not very helpful. Said he knew a lot of Andersons

and could they be any more specific. Confirmed that Morgan was his broker and was doing a good job of managing his investments. Said he'd be delighted to recommend Ralph if someone asked—but nobody had asked him lately, including anybody named Anderson. Just another big, fat stone wall.

"So there you have it, the story according to Ralph Morgan, as augmented by the medical examiner, Lieutenant Hampton, and his industrious crew. I think they've accomplished a fair amount in five days, although you could argue they've really added to the mystery for us—as opposed to helping shed some light on it.

"The 'Great Ellis' will now shut up and turn the floor over to Billy, who can fill you in on how he got involved in all this and what he's been doing till now. Billy . . ."

5

It began to rain again, lightly at first, the drops drumming on the canvas roof of the bar, dimpling the surface of the canal. Big thunderheads were boiling up in the west over Coral Springs and heading our way, with intermittent bolts of lightning just to keep things interesting. Poor old frawgs, I thought, in for a mighty long day.

We snatched up all the luncheon stuff and hustled back into the house just as the skies opened up. MacCardle's Maid Service made short work of the garbage and the dishes. We reassembled in the great room, equipped with a beer each and a truly villainous-looking brier pipe for Ellis, which did a mini-Mount Saint Helens as he lit up.

The storm was directly overhead now—the sky almost black, the lightning crackling all around, and an occasional massive thunderclap that actually shook the house.

Billy began. "Looks like I'll have to compete with Mother Nature for a while, so please be patient and bear with me. I'll do the best I can.

"I've known Laura somewhat longer than I've known Ralph. About three years ago she started showing up at my nine-o'clock service, always in the same seat down front. In a church our size, it doesn't take very long to spot the regulars. Also, she has, or had, the most marvelous singing voice, almost a pure contralto—very much like Judy Collins.

"As a rule, we have coffee and doughnuts in the parish hall after the service. About the fourth or fifth Sunday she came up, introduced herself, and told me she wanted to join Saint Paul's. She had a letter of transfer from her church in New York, Saint Bartholomew's. I have a seminary pal at Saint Bart's, Russell Hayes; I asked if she knew him. She did, slightly, but enough to serve as a link. I told her we'd be delighted to have her join and especially delighted to acquire her voice.

"As time went on, she became more and more involved with the church. It started when I talked her into taking over the women's choir, which was sounding pretty tatty at the time. She did a terrific job with them and they all seemed to enjoy it—our Thursday-night rehearsals had never been so well attended.

"She could and did pinch-hit as organist when Muriel Bannister was away or when the arthritis got to her hands too badly.

"Last spring she helped organize the Strawberry Festival and I doubt it's ever been done as well; at least I know it was the biggest financial success we've ever had. In short, she became one of that handful of people every parish relies on to keep things running smoothly.

"Because of her involvement and our mutual interest in music, I got to know Laura pretty well. Of course, she was a great help to the church, but beyond that, I just liked her as a person.

"Anyway, about a year ago, I sensed that something was troubling her quite badly. She didn't smile as much, her responses lost their old enthusiasm, and her eyes were taking on an almost haunted look. Not the old Laura at all, to the point where I got her aside one day and asked her what was bothering her.

"She told me that she and her husband, Ralph, had been having problems making the marriage work, that things had gone so far they were thinking about separating. I barely knew Ralph then; she'd been successful in dragging him to church on Easter and Christmas—which, unfortunately, is all too common in my line of work—but that was the extent of his participation in church activity.

"As her friend and clergyman, I volunteered my help. After all, marriage counseling does come with the territory, right, Cam?"

Right indeed, chum, remembering vividly the hurt when Lydia and I had gone smash. . . . I'd seen it coming and maybe I could have turned it around, but by then the game didn't seem worth the candle and I just let it reach its natural conclusion.

In her defense—not that The Pearl ever needed much defending—being married to a professional athlete is a tough job. A lot of things combine to make it tough, starting with the annual forced separation of eight weeks that training camp imposes. Half of the long schedule is played out of town—sometimes way out of town—ensuring more separation, plus the impact of occasional jet lag. The winter banquet season and other public relations efforts on behalf of the club subtracts further time from the relationship. Then training camp starts the cycle over again.

The pain doesn't help either. Football players live with pain as a constant, particularly as the body gets older. The bangs and bumps and pulls that used to mend by Tuesday hang on longer and longer, sometimes on into the next Sunday. Pain robs the relationship of many of life's niceties: dinners out, bowling, dancing, even lovemaking. Then there's the privacy or, more properly, the lack thereof. When we went out by ourselves the chances of not being recognized—in a town full of sports nuts like New York—were slim. If we had the Main Man along, which we often did, the chances were zero we'd go through the night without dealing with an endless parade of autograph seekers, well-intentioned fans, and quarrelsome drunks.

Yes, I know the fans pay the salaries, and yes, they are handsome salaries, even if the career often isn't very long. But only the best of fans realize what a price the athlete pays.

I used to have a fantasy in which I got completely stoned,

marched up to the door of a perfectly respectable CPA, hammered on it until he let me in, walked in, and told him in front of his wife and family how he'd blown the Hughes-Moran audit, that his whole firm stank, gave him a fat raspberry, and stalked out. See what I'm driving at?

Anyway, in addition to those pressures, Lydia had to deal with her own competitive nature. After we got married she quit the job at the bank, since (her idea, certainly not mine), "In any respectable, non-emasculating marriage, the man is the sole means of support."

She took all that drive and intellect and tried to channel it into the Junior League, the Daughters of the Confederacy, plus an assortment of volunteer work. It just wasn't enough to soak up that awesome vitality. The upshot was that she would stew over some slight—real or imagined—until it took on the stature of an international incident. What I didn't realize was that the aloofness, the sulks, and the occasional flying crockery were her ways of saying "Notice me, please, notice me." Maybe I thought she was so strong she didn't need help. Maybe I was concentrating so hard on what I was doing that I unconsciously shut her out. Maybe, maybe, maybe. The Amish people have a saying that fits. "Too soon we get old, too late we get smart." In retrospect, I don't give myself very high marks for smarts in understanding The Pearl and what made her tick.

Inevitably, she focused the frustration and hostility on football, "a child's game, played by Cro-Magnon cretins," recalling one of her gentler phrases. Increasingly, she urged me to retire, all too often saying, "I just know I can get Daddy to give you a sales territory and we can leave this dirty smelly city and go live with the nice people."

Of course, I knew that entailed a lifetime diet of Mama, Daddy, Big Lydia, and the Charlotte boar hunters, which I figured would be about as enjoyable as the bubonic plague; but I didn't say that and things just kept drifting downward to a point where we found ourselves icily polite strangers.

The beginning of the end came right after the Rams

game. We'd taken a red-eye charter back from L.A., which
got into Kennedy at five in the morning. By the time I got
home, what I wanted, in order, was twenty-four hours of
sleep, a spell in the Jacuzzi, and a gallon of chicken soup.
What I got was Lydia in her number-one Balenciaga suit—
which I'd once called her game uniform—five pieces of
matched Vuitton luggage in the foyer, and the following pep
talk.

"Welcome back, Mr. Big Man, sorry y'all got creamed
again. You see those things in the hall? Those are Good Ole
Lydia's bags and they're going with Good Ole Lydia to
Charlotte. You stay here with all your little friends and try to
figure out what you want to do when you grow up. If you
need me, though I can't imagine why you would, I'm in the
book under 'V.' If you've got the strength left maybe you
could call the doorman to give me a hand with the bags. Y'all
up to it, Angus?"

I was, but only barely. . . . Then Mr. Big Man dragged
off to bed, slept for twenty- four hours, ate the chicken soup
in the Jacuzzi, and called Gerry Graham.

"I'm not totally surprised. I only met her a few times and
I like Lydia, but I sense she needs a lot of handling, a lot of
careful, constant attention.

"I'm no good at quick fixes or marriage counseling over
the phone. What I can do is give you some things to think
about, which may help the sorting-out process. First of all,
ask yourself if you really gave the marriage a hundred-percent
try. Be truthful with yourself, even if it hurts. If you come to
the conclusion that you didn't give it a hundred percent, then
ask yourself why you didn't. Was it your usual sheer igno-
rance or something deeper; put another way, do you *want* the
marriage to work?

"If you decide you do, then you'd better figure out on
what grounds you want it to work—all or nothing, compro-
mise, who does what for and to whom, including how you
make a living.

"Meanwhile, call Lydia, tell her what you're doing. Ask

her to do the same thing and agree on a time and place to compare notes.

"Best of luck. God bless you both."

Once again, he'd been a friend in need. No moral platitudes, no sanctity-of-the-institution talk, no dime-store theology. Just good, gut-shot questions, plus a framework for self-examination and self-determination.

Three weeks later, after the football season ended, I went to Charlotte to compare notes. Ultimately, The Pearl and I decided we were two nice people who had made an honest mistake that didn't seem fixable, but that we'd always be friends.

Which lasted until she hired Steed Smollert to represent her, a man dedicated to the twin courses of upholding Southern Honor and fleecing about-to-be ex-husbands, both of which he did extremely well.

"Cam, are you listening to all this?"

"Sorry, Padre, wandered off for a second. I'm back." Billy continued. "As I said, they began coming to see me on Tuesday nights—one-hour sessions where the three of us could try working down to the core of their problems. At first, Ralph was most reluctant to come and somewhat uncooperative. But, gradually he began to change and contribute more to the exchanges.

"About three months ago, he called and invited me to dinner, said not to tell Laura, this was to be something between him and me. The evening turned out to be a rather uncomfortable affair. He'd had a lot to drink. Whether that was the cause of it or not, he really came unglued.

"He said Laura was too good for him, never should have married him, deserved more than he could provide. He said he loved Laura, that he really wanted *this* marriage to work, that it was all his fault that things had gone sour. He blamed it on his shyness, said that was why his job wasn't going well, why they had trouble making friends, and even more trouble keeping them. He told me he wanted to change, had to change, but didn't know how.

"I know when I'm over my head, and this was clearly one of those cases. I suggested to Ralph that what he really needed was a different kind of help, that a psychiatrist would be far more effective than I if, in fact, a personality change was what was needed.

"He said he'd thought about that but was afraid, but that he would reconsider. He must have, because he called me a couple of weeks later to say that he had contacted a man in Fort Lauderdale and that he was going to start seeing him right away. I urged him to keep up the marriage counseling sessions, but he said he thought he'd better get himself together first, that he didn't feel he could handle both at once. Probably was a good decision, I don't know.

"In any event, I've come to respect Ralph Morgan. It's awfully hard to do what he is trying to do: holding your ego and and psyche up to that pitiless mirror of self-examination, spotting the flaws, admitting to them, and then going about trying to change them. A tough, tough job for anyone. I'm convinced he did it only because of Laura, wanting to do whatever was necessary to hold the marriage together. That's why, evidence or no evidence, I'm positive there's no way Ralph could have murdered her—it simply goes against the grain of everything he was trying to accomplish."

I suddenly wondered what time it was getting to be. I punched the stem of the Seiko diver's watch and the red numbers flashed 5:45. It didn't seem possible, but we'd chewed up nearly half a day.

"Happy hour, folks," I announced. "Want more of the same or want to switch? I've got everything I believe any sane person would want to drink. Come to think of it, why don't you guys stay for dinner? I've got a London broil, we can microwave some potatoes, Billy can whip up one of his super salads, and there's a jug of California red on ice. What do you say?"

One yes, one no. Dick had to meet his wife at eight at a

political dinner, but thought he could stay until seven-thirty. So I filled the drink orders, broke out some nibbles, and set it all up on the big glass-topped table that flanks the *Lexington*.

Tall, cool one in hand, Billy resumed. "When Dick and I saw him in jail, I was really shocked by Ralph's appearance. It wasn't just the uniform; it was the whole way he carried himself, as if everything had been wrung out of him—a shambling, gray shell of the Ralph Morgan I knew.

"He was concerned principally with two things: notifying Laura's brother, her only living relative, and arranging the funeral. He said in her will Laura had specified cremation. So at least we were spared that part of it. I told him we'd handle the cremation details and suggested a simple memorial service, offered to pick out some hymns I know were Laura's favorites. He was pathetically grateful, tears forming in his eyes when the guard came to take him away.

"Laura's brother, Bobby Evans, lives in Greenville, South Carolina, which is tucked into the northwest corner of the state near the North Carolina border. I know all that because I had never heard of Greenville, so I had to look it up on the map. I called him and broke the news as gently as I could, telling him when and where the memorial service was planned. He told me he had his own plane, which the Boca airport could accommodate easily, said he could be there any time that was convenient for me. I suggested four o'clock the following day and told him I'd meet him at the airport—said I'd undoubtedly be the only one walking around with a funny-looking collar and that I was looking forward to meeting him.

"Meanwhile, Dick's people had done the legal work necessary to get Laura's body released from the morgue, and we had it sent to Donlan's for the cremation. I picked out a simple pewter urn—I thought Laura would have approved—took it over to Donlan's, and then brought it back with me to the church. I ordered some floral arrangements for the altar and told Murial what hymns we would use.

"By that time, it was almost four, so I got in the van and went over to the airport to pick up Bobby.

"I hadn't met him, but Laura had told me a good deal about Bobby, so I wasn't starting from ground zero. Their parents died in a plane crash ten years ago—when Laura was a senior at Smith and Bobby was finishing up his stint in the Army. Over the years they maintained an easy, amiable, hands-off relationship. It wasn't that they didn't love each other, Laura told me; it was just that their lives and interests had been so different.

"Laura had chosen the conventional course—college, a career, finally marriage, and, hopefully, a family. Bobby went a totally different route. Evidently, his whole life has always revolved around automobiles, what makes them tick, how to make them run better and faster, eventually into racing. Laura remembered that in high school, he wasn't much of a student or an athlete, devoted his time instead to fixing cars, performance tuning them, and racing where and whenever he could. Their parents objected violently, but apparently, Bobby was a very independent kid and just kept going his own way.

"His so-so grades weren't good enough to get into any major college, and while he was thinking over what to do, the Army solved the dilemma by drafting him. Laura remembered her parents were secretly relieved, figuring that two years in the Army would mature him, that he would rethink his life-style, get out, and go back to college. In fact, quite the opposite happened.

"As Bobby told me at dinner, he finished his basic training but, unlike so many of us at that time, didn't go to Vietnam. He was sent to Fort Jackson in South Carolina, where the Army, in a rare burst of bureaucratic efficiency, assigned him to the motor pool. There he met a cousin of Richard Petty—the king of stock-car racing—and the two young men became good friends. Petty's cousin took him to a race at Darlington, South Carolina, introduced him to Richard and the other drivers, and got him into Richard's pit area to watch the race on Sunday.

"For the balance of their stay at Fort Jackson, the two

friends followed the NASCAR circuit, going to every race they could, listening on the radio if the track was too far away or if they had drawn weekend duty. He said the two years went by in a flash and by the end of his Army hitch, in his heart, he'd already decided what he wanted to do.

"Then, of course, his parents died and he was free to do as he liked. He was mustered out of the Army, took his severance pay, savings, and what little money his parents left him, and went racing. He calls those early years 'hardscrabble times'—poor equipment, dirt tracks, *never* enough money.

"But he kept racing, started winning, and began to move up steadily, encouraged and advised by Petty, Buddy Baker, Hoss Ellington, Ned Jarrett, and others he'd met on the circuit. He paid his dues, racing Modifieds, then Late-Model Sportsman cars, and finally, five years ago, broke in as a rookie driver on the Winston Grand National Circuit. It's the major league of stock-car racing. He says he isn't in the same class as Petty or Yarborough or Allison and that group, but he has had a couple of wins, thinks he's improving, and, in any event, doing what he's always wanted to do—a pretty good fate for anyone.

"He's a very nice guy and a great storyteller, so the evening passed as well as it could, granted the circumstances. Obviously, he was shocked by Laura's death. He hadn't seen her in two years—remember their relationship—but they'd kept in contact by telephone and the occasional letter. He was most touched when I told him about the scrapbook Laura kept on him and the pride she showed in taking me through it.

"He asked the status of the investigation of her death so far, and I had to tell him there hadn't been much progress, but that it was early and the police were working on it. He wants to get whoever did it, no matter what it takes. He said he couldn't be of much help personally, but that he did have some money if that would be of use to us down the line. Curiously, he never asked once about Ralph Morgan. I finally told him that Ralph was being held, that I'd seen and talked with him, and how broken up Ralph was. Bobby just grunted. I get the impression he doesn't particularly like Ralph, but maybe that's normal for only sister's brother—nobody's good enough.

"We held the memorial service the following day, and the only word I can think of to describe it is 'pathetic.' The flowers were nice, the women's choir sang, and I said some warm things about her, but no one was there. They let Ralph attend, had the decency to allow him to wear regular clothes, unhandcuffed, but the two men who stood on either side of him were clearly not friends of the family. Other than Bobby and two women I don't know, that was it.

"It wasn't at all like your father's funeral, Cam, or any other I've ever gone to—just a sad, strained good-bye, an empty gesture to one who'd been as full of life as Laura. It really depressed me.

"After the service, the two men took Ralph out of the church and the ladies left. I took Bobby to the house for a drink and his bag, drove him to the airport, and saw him off. I put the urn with Laura's ashes in it on a back shelf in my study for safe keeping, but really so that it doesn't remind me of a most unhappy day."

It reminded *me* of one, though, and the part Billy had played in it. . . .

My father died on a golfing holiday in Bermuda. According to his partner, Dad had just canned a twisting little nine-foot touch putt, which gave his team a half on the hole, had reached down to retrieve his ball, and just never got up. A massive cardiovascular infarction—the Big Casino, instant check-out.

Because of his history, I wasn't surprised, but it was still a shock, even though I knew he was living on borrowed time. A couple of years before he'd begun experiencing circulatory problems, had done his usual excellent job of diagnosis, and had taken his problems to Dr. Michael DeBakey, the wizard of Houston.

Of course, Lydia and I went with him, each of us trying

to help the other through the endless hours of tests, prepara-
tion, and, finally, the operation itself. Afterward, DeBakey,
that gifted, no-nonsense little dynamo, had said, charac-
teristically, "I'll give it to you straight up. We did a triple
bypass. We fixed what we could and got the hell out. But, I'm
no car salesman; there aren't any warranties in these cases.
He could live another twenty years or he could go tomorrow.
Just encourage him to welcome every day and use it to its
fullest."

So, I'd known it could happen, but that didn't make it
any easier. What I really felt was cheated—cheated of the
chance to look into the steady, gray eyes and say, "So long,
Dad, thanks for everything. You were a helluva guy and I'm
awfully glad you were my father." All that was left was the
hope that, somehow, he knew all that; but the sense of being
cheated persists, even today.

We buried him out at Saint Mark's Church, around the
corner from the hospital where he'd invested so much of his
life. Dad hadn't been much of a churchgoing person, but I
think he would have liked the service and I know he would
have been touched by the turnout. The whole medical staff
was there, of course, along with the usual crowd of former
patients, all with appropriate expressions of sympathy and
gratitude. We appreciated the mayor's comments, the obitu-
ary in the *Bulletin*, and the floral tributes that poured in from
all over Philadelphia. But the greatest testimony to the man—
what he'd done and who he'd been—came from the little people. Jamming the back of the church were the clerks, the
Gray Ladies, and the orderlies—all come to say one last
good-bye to "Doctor Don." The massive dignity their presence lent was final proof that, indeed, this had been quite a
man.

Afterward, in the now gloomy house on Rittenhouse
Square, I tried to bring some balance to the day. "When you
stop and think about it," I said, "it was a pretty good way to
go. He'd had ten days in the sun with people he liked, doing
what he liked. He was tanned, relaxed, and ready to go back

to work. No long illness, no pain, no time to worry. If somebody offered me the chance to go that way, I'd sign up for it in a minute."

Everyone nodded and even smiled a little. Then Gerry brought us all the way back. "I think you're right, Cam. And from everything I hear about your father, I'm sure the one thing he would want most is for all of you to get back to the business of living. No more moping, no more tears, no sad songs. Instead, good stories, fond memories, and a determination to have at solving the problems that life seems to bring to all of us.

"And speaking of problems, I've got a king-size one on my hands. The Blue-Haired Brigade in my parish have taken to calling me 'Billy.' At first, they thought they were being cute as all get-out, teasing the preacher and all. But it's stuck and I can't shake it. Can you beat that—here I am a graying, dignified man of the cloth, with a perfectly acceptable first name, doomed to go around for the rest of my service known to my flock as Billy Graham. The Big Fella's really testing me with this one."

Well, of course, it was exactly the right touch, delivered with precisely the right timing. We all agreed that *was* a pretty problem but not insurmountable. After all, it did make for a rather catchy name; who were we to stand against the will of his flock. So we tucked the Fearless Friar, duly christened, on his plane for Florida with thanks and with the first real smiles in several weeks.

Billy was talking to me. I'd wandered off again.

"Well, anyway, now you know what we know, Cam. What do *you* think about it all?"

6

Although I had known the question was coming, it still took time to compose what I hoped would be a reasonably intelligent response. After all, they'd dumped a lot on my plate in half a day—a crime, a crew of strangers, and a welter of detail. They'd had a week to try to make sense of it; I'd had five minutes. Look, dummy, stop feeling put upon, I thought, that's what they came here for. There aren't any right or wrong answers, no simple solve, no flash of genius. All they want is your take on a very nasty problem. So I plunged ahead.

"You asked me to be a sounding board and I assume you want a plain, unvarnished opinion—whether or not it's what either one of you would like to hear. Okay. My top-of-mind reaction is that Ralph Morgan looks guilty as hell. On the surface, his story is plausible, but that's all it is, a story. He can't substantiate any part of it and the only person who could is dead. So, his story may be true—every last word of it—but it's got more holes in it than Mario's Swiss cheese.

"On the other hand, the problem, as you outline it, is too simple. Put another way, my hunch is you *don't* know more things than you do know. For example, Laura Morgan may have been a shining light in your church, Billy, but she wasn't above a little afternoon slap and tickle with somebody other than 'beloved husband.' You need to know who it was and whether it concerns the murder or not.

"Laura's character is two-dimensional—devout church-

55

goer and battling housewife. There *has* to be a lot more in between. She *must* have had friends, other activities in her life, people here and elsewhere who could shed more light on understanding her.

"After all, Laura is the key; she's the one who got suddenly taken dead. There must be a reason for it; maybe you have the answer and maybe you don't. Ralph makes an easy patsy and he may well have done it. At this point, if I were a lawyer I'd sure as shootin' rather prosecute than defend.

"But if it *wasn't* Ralph, you don't have the first clue as to who really killed her or why. What could a young housewife with a middle-class background and a religious inclination have done to somebody, somewhere, that warranted murder?

"Billy tells me you think it's hopeless, Dick. You could be right. But before I'd agree with you, it seems to me somebody or bodies have to do an awful lot more digging.

"I think you should do two things: raise all these doubts with Lieutenant Hampton and get the cops going on it, and separately, use some of Bobby Evans's money to hire the best private investigator you can find.

"So there it is, friends. As the commercial says, 'You asked for it, you got it'—MacCardle's take."

Total silence in the room as they thought over what I'd just said. Perhaps they *had* wanted some words of encouragement or a quick fix, but it just wasn't mine to give—not on what I'd heard.

Ellis broke the silence, the words tumbling around his acrid-smelling pipe. "First of all, thanks. You did a good job of listening even *with* an occasional wander. Your summation is quite valid. I understand why Billy thought it would be a good idea to get together. I'll only take issue with you on two points. Number one, I *will* raise all the doubts with Wade Hampton. But I know what pressures these people are under and how shorthanded they are. If I had to guess—and that's often what I get paid to do—I'd guess that Hampton thinks he has enough right now to recommend going to trial. He's a good cop, but he's got a lot to do. His evidence is circumstantial, sure, but all the signs point against Morgan. So I wouldn't count on much more effort from them.

"Number two, the private investigator thing. I don't know a reputable P.I. who would touch this one with a ten-foot pole. You're dead right. We *don't* have a clue and there is a lot of digging to be done, with not much time to do it. The chance of failure is enormous, and failure to a P.I. means he couldn't get a job as a school crossing guard.

"The less reputable ones—not that we'd want them— would just two-hundred-dollar-a-day us until Ralph got sent off to Raiford, or worse, this being a capital punishment state. So that's out.

"What I think we need is someone who knows the details of the case, has the time to do the digging we agree needs doing, and who won't be affected if the digging doesn't produce. Billy doesn't have the time. I don't either and—I know it sounds cynical—I'm not sure I want to stake my reputation on defending Ralph Morgan, at least not now. It strikes me, particularly after this afternoon, that *you* fit that bill rather well. Not as a private investigator, of course, more in the line of being our arms and legs. We would cover any costs involved, and if you fail, so what?—at least you tried. Think it over, Cam. Believe me, I'll understand if you turn it down. If you do decide to go ahead, please let me know in a day or so, so that we can do the paper work and I can clear it with Lieutenant Hampton, who neither one of us needs to cross.

"Look here! It's just past seven-thirty. I'd better call a cab if I want to meet Susan on time."

So I called Cooney's Cab—"Twenty-Four Hour Service, Radio Dispatched, Reliability Our Promise"—and we chatted idly while we waited. As the cab pulled up and I opened the front door for him, Dick said, "Thanks again for listening. It was a profitable day for me. Win, lose, or draw, it was good to see you again." And he went off in search of Susan.

Billy and I polished off the steak and potatoes, along with salad à la Graham and a truly vicious loaf of garlic bread, making an impressive dent in a jug of California red in the process.

We talked about many things during dinner, but inevitably we would come back to the Morgans and to the proposal Ellis had made. There was some logic to it—I'd grant him that—although it seemed a logic born mostly out of lack of options. I had so many doubts, and the responsibility involved seemed overwhelming. I wouldn't be affected if we failed, Dick had said. That was true—up to a point. But if we failed, Ralph Morgan was sure as hell going to be affected—innocent or no—and nobody I knew was about to elect MacCardle to the Detectives' Hall of Fame.

Over the last of the coffee, Billy didn't make the decision any easier, looking across the table, saying, "Angus, I don't mean to sound preachery, but the Morgans—both of them— are part of my parish and my ministry. I must help them any way I can or else walk away from all the reasons I became a priest.

"Ralph Morgan has his faults, God knows, but I just don't believe he killed Laura—I don't think it's in him. Without us, he's all alone in the world, facing a bigger problem than you and I have ever faced between us.

"Laura Morgan wasn't perfect either—nobody is—but she was a great help to my church and she was my friend. If we don't find out who really killed her, no matter who it is, Laura will always be what she is to me now—an unfulfilled responsibility, a debt I have to honor. If I let it go by default I won't be able to live with myself, Angus; of all people you can understand that."

So I said I'd think about it carefully, shooed him out the door, cleaned up the galley, and went off to bed.

It had been a very long day, make no bones about it.

I couldn't get to sleep at all, remembering Billy's anxious face and the magic word, the tacit appeal for help.

Why me, I thought, why load all this grief on me—then realized how childishly selfish that sounded, remembering the

Day of the Knee and the events that followed, which were the reasons I was now here in Florida. I'd been selfish then, too.

The Day of the Knee. Football players dread it every time they step onto a field. A fortunate few never get it. Even less get one and get over it. For most, the Day of the Knee was the end of the sporting life.

I was in my seventh year with the club, and for the first time, we were respectable—with a real shot at making the playoffs, maybe even the Super Bowl.

We'd been running a stutter step curl pattern under a rookie cornerback all afternoon. He was giving us the two-steps, the seven-yarders, and the Main Man was delighted to take them. Once again, I came off the line, counted the steps, turned for the ball . . . and woke up in the hospital peering past some strange contraption in my mouth at Dr. Sterne, our ortho guy, and a very frightened-looking nurse.

"Jesus, God, Cam, you had us half scared to death. You got hit so hard it knocked your hat off. By the time I got there your eyes were rolling around and your head was jerking back and forth; if you'd been a horse I think I would have shot you. That thing in your mouth was to keep you from swallowing your tongue. I think we can take that out now, Cooper. You have two problems: a deep concussion and a knee that looks like seven pounds of cement in a five-pound sack. We pulled all the skull films in the training room while you were out, then we brought you here. I looked at the films on the way in. You should be fine, although you're gonna have a helluva headache for the next two days and a real pair of shiners.

"About the knee, I just don't know. For sure they tore up that remedial process we did two years ago, probably added some damage of their own. We'll do the arthroscope work tonight, and tomorrow we can talk. Meanwhile, Cooper and her relief have some stuff that will keep you from jumping out of your skin without knocking you out—I want you awake so we can make sure the skull films are right.

"See you later . . . I'm sorry, Cam."

Dr. Sterne is a big, jowly man who goes through life with such a permanently lugubrious look the troops call him Snoopy—behind his back, of course, since he's a very nice guy.

I was glad to see Snoopy, both because it took some of the fear out of waking up in a hospital unexpectedly and because he was familiar with my knee. But I didn't like what he was saying, or his tone of voice. It looked like a very long night.

It was—a night full of pain and self-doubt, of helplessness and fear. The worst fear is not of something physical, not of fire or knife or bullet; the worst fear is the fear of the unknown. Because you can't do anything about it, it grows and grows in the darkness until you want to scream for help. I know a woman who had a mastectomy; she told me the worst part of the ordeal was getting it over with—one way or the other—so that tangible problems could replace the horrors of the mind's invention. I began to understand what she had been saying.

The early morning wasn't any better, although at least it had daylight and human traffic and an end to the night sweats. I pecked at the standard hospital subhuman breakfast and tested the thin, lukewarm coffee—blech!

They brought me the papers, which had good news—we won—and bad news—speculation on my knee and my future. One of the subheads said it all, MACCARDLE OUT FOR SEASON—AT LEAST. Wonderful.

Snoopy came by at ten, looking, if possible, even more mournful than ever. "It isn't good, Cam. All the old damage is back plus a stellate fracture of the patella and an internal sublunar cartilage that looks like it's been through a shredder. With good surgical results and extensive rehabilitation, I think you'll recover seventy-five to eighty percent effectiveness. You'll be able to get around all right, but I'm afraid that's it for football."

I argued that guys had come back before from this kind of thing: Frederickson, Sayers, Kyle Rote, a lot of them. I suggested we bring in Dr. Karlan from Los Angeles, whose work in this specialty had achieved spectacular results.

Snoopy shook his head. "Bob's *already* involved. We sent our findings to him by computer last night. I just got off the phone with him. The seventy-five percent number is his. Even if you did beat the odds on this one, you'd be risking some form of permanent synovitis, maybe arthritis. It isn't worth it. You're too young to be a cripple."

So, there it was. Ball game. End of the road. No options, no choices. A sad-eyed man, in measured words, telling me my world, as I knew it, had just ended. Irrationally, the old sailor's hornpipe had popped into my mind. "What do you do with a washed-up ballplayer, ear-lie in the morning?"

I don't remember much about the days after the operation. A shrink friend of mine later told me it's a process called sublimation, the mind's ability to simply suppress things it doesn't want to face.

I remember Snoopy coming by, smiling for once, to tell me the operation had been as successful as they could have hoped. Of course, the troops dropped in, frequently at first, less and less as the needs of their own lives reclaimed them. I had two very uncomfortable meetings with the press. The second wound up with me in tears, and after that they left me alone. I got a telephone call from Lydia that depressed me so badly I asked the nurse to take the phone out. I decided to take a crack at the world dropout record, although it wasn't a truly conscious decision at the time.

I might have made it, too, except for Billy. He came stalking in one morning, just as I was deciding whether the next three hours would be better spent on the right side or the left, and he really let me have it.

"MacCardle, you're nothing but a waste of time—to your fans, to the people who love you, to yourself. And you're a monumental disappointment to me"

I mumbled something about how his bedside manner could stand improvement, but I don't think he even heard me.

"The nurses tell me there's a stack of unopened telegrams and letters out there big enough to choke a dinosaur. I know you turned off the phone because I've tried to get you at least a dozen times. Worst of all, the doctor told me you won't even talk about rehabilitation.

"You big, dumb, jerk. Lying there playing lima bean. Hoping it will all go away. Crying about things you can't change. It's a wonder you're not sucking your thumb."

I sat up and did my best to glare him out the window. No use.

"You have a college degree and a head that was designed to do more than attract concussions. You had six and a half wonderful years in the Bigs that nobody can take away from you. You've made friends and business contacts all over the United States. Except for one lousy knee, you have everything else God issued you, all in good working order. You can do almost anything you want, teach, coach, sell things, own a little business, you name it. You don't even have to work for a living. With the pension and what your father left you, you don't have to lift a hand for the rest of your miserable life. I should feel sorry for you? Hah!"

I thought he'd wound down by then, and he was starting to get to me. "Yeah, but," I said eloquently.

"No 'but,' Angus. No 'ifs,' no 'maybes,' no 'might-have-beens.' Here's what we're going to *do*. Assuming you are willing to give up your career as a veggie, you get the doctors to give you a step-by-step written program on rehabilitating the knee. Then you check out of this snuggery, pack your bags, and come to Florida. I've got room at the house—it's about a mile from the water.

"There we put you through the whole rehab program. If you thought Parris Island was fun, you ain't seen nothin' yet. After that and only after that, we'll talk about what you do with the rest of your life.

"Call me when you've made up your so-called mind."

On that note he left. Five feet six of quivering indignation. Truth be told, I was ready to go with him, but we must maintain appearances, so I waited a couple of days and then did exactly what he proposed.

Much later Billy would tell me what it had cost him to make that speech, but there's no question it was the right medicine at the right time. It's made all the difference in the world to me.

I smiled to myself and dropped off to sleep.

I woke up to blazing sunshine and the promise of a lovely day—a welcome change from the rain. I lay in bed for a while, all of yesterday's happenings still buzzing around in my mind. A run on the beach should fix that, I thought, so I got up, pulled on bathing trunks and polo shirt, scuffed into the Topsiders, got in the car, and headed north.

I was pretty sure I knew what I was going to do, but running always seems to help me think, and this was something not to be rushed into, for certain.

The beach just below Delray is almost always guaranteed to be deserted at this hour of the morning, which is why I favor it; today was no exception. Yesterday's storm activity had moved out to sea, combining with the offshore reef formation to produce some monstrous waves.

So I ran on the hard-packed sand at the water's edge, the gulls circling and mewing overhead, the surf producing a low, continuous roar. As the waves crashed ahead of me, they threw off sheets of spume, which caught the sunlight, creating a never-ending series of rainbows that stretched as far as I could see.

Truly a keeper day, I thought, one to store in the memory bank for retrieval when the weather or the mood turned sour. The solitude of the beach and the beauty produced by the waves made me recall the old sailors creed, "Lord, thy sea is so vast and my craft so frail." Metaphysics in the morning, MacCardle, will wonders never cease?

Two miles up, two miles back, and the sorting-out process was completed. I trudged up the steep dunes to the road, got in the car, and started home, whistling softly. Suddenly realized *what* I was whistling and hoped, wryly, that my mind wasn't trying to send a subconscious message—an old Stephen Sondheim classic—"Send in the Clowns."

Stopped at the traffic light on A1-A just below my Hillsboro Road crossover, I saw a bumper sticker that really made my day. Ordinarily I'm not much for bumper stickers and I don't understand why people put them on their cars. Like "Visit Lookout Mountain," "WQRS FM Radio 101.5," "Olympic Beer Drinking Team"—ugly, ug-lee. But this one was a classic. Done like a strip of bunting, in red, white, and blue, it said, "Will the Last American Leaving Miami Please Bring the Flag?" I laughed all the way home.

I pulled into the driveway, scooped up the morning paper, went on inside, and put the coffee on. Took a long, hot shower, then shaved, wiping the steam from the mirror. Looked at my reflection, made an imaginary pistol out of thumb and forefinger, pointed it at me, and said, "Look out Ellery Queen, move over Mike Hammer. Eat your heart out Travis McGee—here comes MacCardle."

To do *what*, I thought soberly. Right now everything's an unknown—including you. Lines from a Robert Frost poem jumped out.

> The woods are lovely, dark and deep.
> But I have promises to keep,
> And miles to go before I sleep,
> And miles to go before I sleep.

But the spirit of the day would not be denied. Okay, so you're no ace sleuth, I thought. You *can* be arms and legs, hopefully a mind as well. You *can* go out there and do the best you know how. They can't shoot you for *trying*.

So I finished shaving, got dressed, poured the coffee, called Billy, and told him to count me in, such as I was. I hadn't expected an effusive reaction and I didn't get one. Billy simply said, "Thank you, Angus. God bless you." It was more than enough.

7

Wednesday-afternoon meeting—Ellis, me, and Lieutenant Hampton—in Hampton's office. It looked exactly like what I had always imagined a top cop's office *would* look like: black-and-white lineoleum tile on the floor, a battered, gunmetal gray steel desk and matching file cabinet, a sparsely upholstered metal desk chair on casters, and two armless wooden chairs for visitors.

The American flag, cased in a standard, stood in one corner behind his desk; in the other corner was the flag of the State of Florida. An enormous map of the city of Cypress Beach was centered between the flags, covering the majority of the wall directly behind the desk. The one window, made of that glass imbedded with chicken wire, looked out onto an asphalt, fenced-in compound for police vehicle maintenance. There were no pictures on the other institutional-gray walls, no signs of personal imprint anywhere in the office.

The only splash of color in the room was a reminder of the season, a miniature wreath with a bell and red ribbon, scotch-taped to the doorframe, looking as out of place as a rose on the walls of the Kremlin.

A wooden sign, next to the nameplate on the corner of his desk away from the three-tiered out/in/pending box, summed it up nicely. B-BRIEF & B-GONE it said.

Clearly a no-frills, no-fripperies place to get things done, a statement all by itself, and an office whose personality exactly matched that of its occupant. Wade Hampton was a massive man—as tall as I and forty pounds heavier, though he carried the weight well. He looked very much like a younger version of Anthony Quinn. The hooded, almost black eyes suggested that somewhere back in the Hampton line they might have thrown in a little Cherokee for seasoning. There was a touch of gray at the temples in the dark hair, and I pegged him as late thirties, maybe early forties. The uniform was clean and sharply pressed, the military creases in the back of his shirt describing three precisely parallel lines. Everything that was leather shone, all the metal glistened. A well-cared-for machine, I thought, oiled and ready to go. Ellis had been dead on. This was definitely not a man to cross.

Dick had a file on Hampton, which I'd read yesterday, noting he'd spent four years in the Marine Corps. After the introductions, in my best Dale Carnegie manner, I'd run several do-you-knows by him, but his answers displayed such a total lack of interest that I just shut up and let Ellis run the meeting.

"Wade, first off, 'preciate you seeing us so promptly," Dick began. "I know y'all are real busy, so we'll just be as brief as we can, hear?"

What's with the sudden backwoodsiana? I wondered. Then I realized Ellis was nervous and found myself wondering why.

"The purpose of this lil' get-together is twofold," he continued. "To introduce Mr. Cam MacCardle to you, personal-like, and then to talk about the status of the Morgan thing.

"Like I told you on the phone, this ole boy is going to work for me, kinda on a project basis, you might say, and I thank you for any and all help you and your folks can give him.

"Now, what can y'all tell us about your plans for my good client, Mr. Morgan?"

Hampton looked at both of us with a flat, unwavering stare and told us, very politely, that while things are never simple in this life and while there was always the *chance* of extenuating circumstances and new evidence, the deal, in his words, looked open and shut.

Specifically, he said, "When I am faced with making decisions of this nature, I start by taking a pad of legal-size paper—like this here—and making three columns on it: 'What We Know,' 'What We Think We Know,' 'What We Would Like To Know.' I have taken all the evidence our people have compiled to date and put it into the appropriate columns. Rather than reading it to you, I will simply show you the actual summation I used."

He turned the pad around and pushed it across the desk to us. We pulled our chairs up to the edge of the desk, Dick put on his glasses, and we read it together.

Under the "What We Know" column, he had written:

1. We know that Laura Evans Morgan is dead.
2. We know she did not die by her own hand.
3. We know how, where, and approximately when she was killed.
4. We can document Mr. Morgan's presence at his residence within the time frame established by the M.E. as her time of death.
5. We cannot account for Mr. Morgan's whereabouts from 1:00 P.M. to 2:15 P.M.
6. We know Mrs. Morgan had sexual relations with a person or persons unknown—but not her husband—on the afternoon of the day of her death.
7. We know that Mr. and Mrs. Morgan were not getting along well and, in fact, were given to heated arguments.
8. We can neither prove nor disprove that Mr. Morgan received that telephone call from his wife as he maintains. We can, however, demonstrate that the restaurant referred to, the man Anderson, and the notes Morgan claims he took of the conversation do not exist.
9. For his part, Mr. Morgan cannot substantiate his whereabouts for three periods of time: 1:00 P.M. to 2:15 P.M.;

5:30 until shortly after 7:00; from then until 9:14, when Officers Randolph and Serkin responded to Mr. Morgan's telephone call.

10. We know there were no signs of breaking and entering or any sort of struggle whatever.

The "What We Think We Know" column was much shorter:

1. The security apparatus on the front door—double deadbolt locks, a chain, and a peephole—suggests wariness of strangers by at least one of the Morgans. Presumably that would be Mrs. Morgan, granted she was often at home all day alone.

2. We can assume that, granted no physical signs of breaking or entering or struggle, the killer was a person well known by Mrs. Morgan—someone whom she would admit to her house freely or someone who had a key.

3. We can assume the murder was a crime of passion and not accomplished for financial reward, granted her lack of personal assets and absent any sign of robbery.

4. We do not know whether Mr. Morgan was aware of his wife's infidelity or infidelities. We can assume that if he had become aware, it could have provided ample cause for Mr. Morgan to commit such a crime of passion.

The "What We Would Like To Know" column had only two entries:

1. Instead of lunching alone, as he claims, did Mr. Morgan, in fact, go home midday Monday? Did he catch his wife, either directly or in a compromising situation, return that evening to confront her, and, in the confrontation, kill Mrs. Morgan?

2. Why doesn't Mr. Ralph Morgan give up on his tale of the telephone call and the mysterious stranger and confess that he did, in fact, murder his wife?

We finished the reading, glumly, and sat back in our chairs. Hampton made a steeple of his fingers, lowered his chin onto the steeple, and said, "Next steps, gentlemen? I don't see where I have much of a choice. I have a dead woman on my hands. I have a suspect who had sufficient time in which to murder her, undetected. The same suspect had some reason, and perhaps more than some reason, to perpetrate the murder. The same suspect cannot account for his whereabouts at the time of the murder, except through a story that cannot be substantiated, ever, by anyone.

"I have no other suspects, nor reason to believe they will materialize. Mr. Morgan has been properly arraigned. I have recommended to the district attorney's people that he be detained here until his trial, at which time he will, I have no doubt, be convicted of murder in the first degree of his wife, Laura Evans Morgan. Further, I have recommended that no bail bond be available to Mr. Morgan, that he be held in formal custody until and including his trial.

"Granted current court calendars, I would estimate he has about two months to raise further evidence or corroboration of his alibi. In cases like this, the district attorney likes to move quickly. It saves the taxpayers money. Failing that, frankly, I don't think he has a chance, Mr. Ellis. As an admirer of yours, which I am, I would urge you to stay away from this one. If you choose not to, I can assure you and Mr. MacCardle of this department's complete cooperation. Speaking for the district attorney, I can also assure you that Mr. Morgan will receive a fair and honest trial. I must tell you, however, that we are satisfied that Mr. Morgan is indeed the murderer."

"Lieutenant, I'm sure you realize that all of this so-called evidence is highly circumstantial."

Hampton stood up, his face shadowed by the light of the old-fashioned gooseneck lamp on his desk. "Mr. Ellis, I never mentioned the word 'evidence'; I simply described the details of this case as we know them, including the possibility of Mr. Morgan's being able to perpetrate the crime in the time periods in which he cannot prove where he was.

"Circumstantial? If you mean do we have an eyewitness who physically saw Mr. Morgan strangle his wife, the answer, obviously, is no. Granted the facts in our possession, however, which side of the case would you like to argue, Counselor? If you had your druthers, that is.

"Now if you will excuse me, we all have things to do and never enough time to do them. While it may seem inappropriate in these surroundings, I wish you and all of yours a Merry Christmas."

The meeting was over. Somehow, I felt we had been dismissed—politely but firmly.

We left Lieutenant Hampton's office silently, not looking at each other, walked through the clutter and din of the dayroom, down the short flight of stairs, through the main doors of the building, out onto the street. We turned left and started walking—still in silence. Finally, Ellis stopped and turned to me. "I don't know about you, but I could use a drink. As I recall, there's a place about two blocks from here called the Pelican's Roost. It's not the fanciest bar in the world, but it's quiet."

I'd been about to suggest a drink myself, so I simply nodded and followed along. We walked in, found a booth in the back, and sat. The Roost was better than Dick had described, almost out of place for this side of town: no jukebox or arcade games or cute mottoes on the wall; clean tableclothes, warm lights, Muzak set at an acceptable level; and a waitress who appeared quickly, without giving the impression that we were just another burden to be dealt with in the course of her endless day.

We gave her our order: beer for me, a very dry, double Beefeater martini on the rocks with no vegetables, please, for Ellis. The drinks came and I awarded the Pelican another star—a frosted mug for my beer, a tumbler the size of a small fishbowl for Dick, and a dish of mixed nuts complete with a stack of cocktail napkins so that your fingers didn't get greasy. Nicely done.

Dick made half the martini disappear in a single gulp,

setting the tumbler down and shaking his head as the gin took a whack at his nervous system. "Hmmmm, boy that's good—just like broken glass."

I smiled, but I had a question that had been gnawing away at me since the beginning of our session with Hampton, and I had to know the answer.

"Dick, please excuse the rudeness, but what was that mush-mouth act in Hampton's office all about? For a minute there I thought you were going to scuff your feet and pull your forelock."

He looked over, ruefully. "Yeah, I know, the hotshot trial lawyer and all. I don't know what it is about that man—at least in his office—but he makes me feel like the schoolboy who broke the window, trying to explain to the principal that it was an accident. Call it protective coloration, that good-ole-boy number. Anyway, you have to admit he's a pretty imposing guy."

I did have to admit that and I agreed with Dick's schoolboy analogy, my own feeling of being dismissed still rankling somewhat.

"He's some piece of work, all right, and by the way, so are you, Counselor; your guess was right on the button as to where the police would stand and what we could expect from them. You think he meant it when he promised full cooperation with us?"

"I think he did. Hampton's tough, but he's honest and he's realistic. He obviously thinks he has enough to go on right now, enough so he's not going to spend any more time looking into it. On the other hand, he wants to make sure the guilty party—whether it's Ralph or not—takes the fall. He'll help where he can. But, we're going to play it absolutely straight with him. No terrific little scams like James Garner does on television; the man is no buffoon. We tell him what we're going to do and why, then we tell him what we did—although we may want to allow for a bit of judicious editing. Whatever you find out, bring it back to me and we'll figure out the best way of serving it up to the good lieutenant."

That sounded fine to me; besides clarifying my responsibilities, it also described a role in which I'd feel comfortable. All my life I've been painfully honest—not necessarily as a sign of great character, more because I'm just too lazy to try to keep more than one set of mental books. Fake business cards, diguised voices, and assumed characters were out of my league—best left to the big kids and heroes of improbable fiction.

"Okay with me, Counselor, in fact more than okay. Speaking of telling Hampton about what we're doing, it seems to me it's time I met Ralph Morgan. Hampton figures we've got about two months. If he's right, that's not a whole lot of time, even for a supersleuth of my caliber. I need to spend at least a half a day with him just to get us started. How quickly do you think you can set it up?"

Dick finished the last of his martini, looked at me ruefully, and said, "Guess you're not up to it tonight, eh? Didn't think so. Let's try for first thing in the morning. I'll have my gal call over there now and set it up. Check with me tonight."

So, I paid the check, adding a tip that brought another smile from the friendly waitress, and drove home wrapped in a cloud of self-doubt. More than ever, I didn't like Ralph Morgan's chances worth a whit. More than ever, I wondered what in the world I was bringing to this party. Reality was the cold efficiency of Hampton's office, the steady stacking of the chips on the wrong side—at least wrong from Ralph Morgan's point of view.

Think positively, kiddo; tomorrow you can get to hear his side of it. There has to be something we can go on. This ball game isn't over yet, never mind the score.

But . . . it hadn't been a very promising beginning.

8

Getting dressed next morning posed its own set of new challenges. I mean, what does the average supersleuth wear to an investigation? I decided that since I didn't have the foggiest idea, I'd settle on Establishment Informal, what The Pearl used to call Aging Ivy. Tropical-weight gray worsted trousers, button-down shirt, regimental stripe tie. Black, calf-length socks, Bally loafers, topped with a featherweight navy-blue blazer. Neat but not gaudy.

On yesterday's trip I had acquired two of the tools of my new trade: a small, six-ring, loose-leaf notebook with lined paper and a folding map of Broward and southern Palm Beach counties. Maps are one of the little things in life that defeat me, not reading them—the Marine Corps had taken care of that—but in trying to refold them into something that begins to approximate their original form. My new map had fought me tooth and nail yesterday afternoon—and won, as usual—and was now sitting on the coffee table looking like a slightly dog-eared version of the New York City Yellow Pages.

I drank the last of the coffee, set the air conditioning on low cycle, locked up, and got in the car. Notebook in the blazer pocket, rebellious map crammed into the glove compartment, I set off for Cypress Beach, hoping that I looked a great deal more confident than I felt.

Last night Ellis had said nine o'clock sharp—I could guess where the *sharp* part had come from. Best get off on the right foot, boy. I actually got to the building at quarter of, walked around the block twice, and went in at 8:55.

A Sergeant Serkin was waiting for me outside Hampton's office, doing a credible imitation of a well-dressed Washington Monument. My God, I thought, he's even bigger than Hampton; maybe they hire them by size around here. The name Serkin was vaguely familiar, then I remembered the last part of our meeting with Lieutenant Hampton. Serkin must be the sergeant part of the team that had responded to Ralph Morgan's call the night Laura was killed.

"You MacCardle?" he asked.

I nodded.

"Right on the dot, I see. That's good—the lieutenant don't hold much with being late. You working with that lawyer, Ellis, huh? Can't say I envy you or him—or Morgan neither, come to think of it. Well, let's be going, time's wasting."

I followed him toward what I judged was the back of the building, through a maze of corridors and turns. Should have dropped bread crumbs, I thought inanely; never get back outside without a trained guide.

Finally, Serkin stopped at a door marked INTERROGATION ROOM 2, opened the door, and motioned me in. If Hampton's office had been Spartan, this one was truly bare bones: a small room with no windows, dominated by a large scarred wooden desk in the center, chairs of indeterminate age and origin ranked around it. An equally battered wooden table sat off to the side, on which sat a carafe, a stack of mugs, and a bowl containing packets of sugar and dry creamer.

"This is first-cabin treatment, MacCardle; the boss must really like you people. Generally, you only get to see prisoners in the visiting room, at regular visiting hours. You even got coffee. Like I say, first-cabin all the way."

In my best Perry Mason fashion I pointed out that Morgan had been arraigned not convicted, but Serkin just shrugged.

"Yeah, well, for now maybe. Look, here's the score. You

sit here, Morgan sits yonder, where the guard can keep an eye on him through that little window in the door. You want anything, you push this buzzer—it's connected to the guard's desk outside. I'll be back at twelve to get you; want to leave earlier, just push the button. Clear?"

Clear. All too clear, at least as far as Serkin was concerned. Open and shut. Matter of time. Move on to the next one, stop wasting the taxpayers' money.

Still, it had been nice of Lieutenant Hampton to think of coffee; maybe he and Ellis were closer than I thought, certainly closer than Dick's nervousness the other day would suggest. I went over to the table, poured a mug of coffee, took it to my Serkin-assigned place, and sat, waiting for the guard to bring Ralph Morgan.

Which happened, typically, right after I sat down. Motorists change lanes just as the lane they are in starts moving; smokers light cigarettes and the No Smoking light goes on in the plane; the telephone stops ringing just as you come belting in from outside to get it. Uncanny.

The door opened and in came Morgan, the guard two steps behind him, holding a riot gun at a very correct port arms. He motioned Morgan to sit down, told me he assumed Sergeant Serkin had outlined the proper procedure, reminded me about the buzzer, turned, and left, the door closing behind him as he assumed his post outside.

My first impressions of Ralph Morgan were not particularly encouraging. He sat huddled in his chair, shoulders hunched forward as though awaiting a blow, his face as gray as the oversize, washed-out prison uniform shirt he wore. Everything about him, slack mouth, dull gaze, hands picking at each other nervously on the tabletop, said, "Okay, you win, I give up." Not encouraging at all.

When he spoke, it was like some sad parody of past, more pleasant business encounters he'd had. "Mr. MacCardle, first of all, thank you for coming. I'm sorry about the surroundings, not our usual practice at all, I assure you. At least we won't be bothered by telephones ringing; I suppose that's a blessing anyway, eh?"

My God, I thought, this guy's about to go over the edge; we're going to lose this one before we start. So I jumped up, put my hands together in the form of a T, and said sharply, "Hold it, Ralph, time out, we're going the wrong way."

In slightly softer tones I added, "Look, we're not in your office and I don't want my portfolio examined. This is a *jail*. You're being held for *murder*. I'm here to help."

Finally, in a normal voice, I said, "Let's start over again. We're on your side, but we need a lot of information in not much time. So, let's make it Cam and Ralph from now on. Got it?"

He nodded and I was relieved to see that his eyes had lost some of the glazed-over look, saw there were two splotches of color in his cheeks. I guess I hit a nerve.

His voice regained some strength. "Got it. I know where I am and I know why—at least I think I do. It's just been such a shock: Laura, jail—I've never even gotten a parking ticket—in strange clothes, in a cell, I mean, put yourself my place."

I gestured at the coffee and he nodded. I walked over and poured a cup. Added sugar as requested and brought it over to him, suggesting he keep it and his hands where the guard could see them.

"That's another thing, the guards. Did you see that guy with the riot gun? For me? I'm just a stockbroker trying to make a living, not John Dillinger. Guards, for heaven's sake."

"Don't forget they think you killed her. An open-and-shut deal. You can't exactly expect kid-glove treatment."

"It's not that they're treating me badly. They're all being very polite; even the food isn't all that bad. It's the not knowing what's going on or where to turn to that's driving me crazy. The nights are the worst. I see her lying there, so helpless, violated. I go over and over in my mind what happened and I still can't make sense of it. Laura gone. Accusing me. No one to talk to, no one to listen, no one to believe that

what I'm saying is true. I can't stand it; it's the worst thing
I've ever gone through."

I told him I could understand how he felt and that he was
doing a remarkable job of holding up—which wasn't exactly
true, but I figured he could use all the confidence he could
get. I told him about the preliminary investigation—except
for the sex thing—how Ellis, Billy and I got involved, and
where we were to date—which was nowhere. I told him *he*
was the key to the whole thing, that without him there wasn't
any way to ever find out who killed Laura. I urged him to
dredge up everything and anything he thought might be even
remotely helpful to understanding Laura better and why anyone would want to kill her.

"Ralph, we need a little organization. Let's try a sort of
agenda. Three parts. Some questions on where you were that
day. Whatever background you can give me on Laura. Finally, any people you can think of who might be helpful to us.
Okay?"

He was leaning forward, shoulders knotted, fists on the
table. When he looked at me his eyes were clear and steady.
Maybe this one's a fighter after all, I thought. Maybe I'd
pushed the right button.

"I'll do whatever you fellows say. I loved her. I want to
know who took her away from me, see whoever killed her get
what's coming to them. You have to believe I didn't do it; it's
the last thing on earth I'd even think of."

"What's important is what *they* believe. There are some
pretty impressive gaps in your story. We have to try to fill
them. Let's take the deli, for example. Was anybody you
know in there?"

"No. I don't know. I don't remember. I just wanted to
get my sandwich and go think."

"How about the counter man. Would he recognize you?"

"You can ask. I doubt it, though. It's a high turnover
kind of place. Order, pay, go. I don't know anybody by
name, don't go there that often."

"Did you order anything they might remember? Special sandwich? Something offbeat to drink?"

"How about a ham on rye and a Coke? Not very helpful, I guess."

"No. Okay, scratch that idea for now. How about the park? See anybody there you knew?"

"If I had, I would have gone somewhere else. I just wanted to be by myself. Think. Get Laura to stop being angry with me. Besides, it was kinda late for lunch. I don't recall seeing anyone."

"Anything happen while you were there? Traffic accident, Goodyear blimp come overhead, anything that could place you there?"

"Look, I know where you're going and I'm trying to help. But you have to understand, my mind was a million miles away. Plus, I never dreamed I'd have to substantiate where I was. You see?"

"*Sure* I see. Just looking for anything that might help. You said the office was empty when you left. A Mrs. Hillson says she saw you leave your condo around seven. Anyone see you when you came in?"

"No, and like I told the police, I don't remember seeing Hillson either."

"Okay, okay. Let's skip to the restaurant search part. That's two hours and change they think you can't account for. Same deal—anybody see you, you see anybody, anything that can pinpoint you?"

"I've been over that ground a hundred times. I know it sounds fishy, but it's true, every word. I swear it."

"Nothing? How about directions; you stop and ask anyone?"

"I had the directions. Laura gave them to me on the phone. Directions were fine. The problem was the place didn't exist."

"What did you do with the directions?"

"I was so upset I wadded up the paper and threw it as far

as I could. What's the use anyway? They'd probably say I faked them."

"Don't give up. Just hang in. How about when you got back to the condominium? Anyone see you come in?"

"No. I remember how quiet it was. One of those soft nights, with all the stars out. Then . . . I walked into that nightmare, I. . ."

"Steady. Keep thinking about it. Maybe it will come to you. Give it a chance. Somebody might have seen you. You must have seen somebody, something. You think about it. Want more coffee?"

"Please."

I got his cup, refilled it, brought it over to him, went back to my side of the table, and sat—all in a sort of a slow motion so the guard wouldn't get nervous.

"Let's move down the agenda. Tell me everything you know about Laura, where she comes from, how you met, what you did together, that kind of thing. Don't leave anything out—I'll decide later what's useful and what isn't."

In the beginning the words came slowly, painfully—understandable granted the subject he was talking about. I kept at him, coaching, prodding, drawing him out, helping him over the worst of the rough spots. After a time it got easier for him; in the end the thoughts and words were flowing quite naturally.

"Laura and I met in Florida," he began. "I don't know a great deal about her before then because she never talked about it much. She was twenty-two when she graduated from Smith. Her parents had died earlier that year—they left her some money, but she still had to work for a living. She wasn't all that sure what she wanted to do. Apparently, her father's best friend was an advertising executive in one of the big New York agencies—J. Walter Thompson—so she went to talk to the personnel people there. Evidently, she must have done well with them, and I'm sure his endorsement helped. She got a job as a media trainee.

"It was an exciting place to be, a great experience for a kid fresh out of college. I'm not sure what media departments do, but Laura said her job involved calling CBS and Time, Inc.—really *all* the networks and magazines—plus lunches and meetings with people she'd only read or heard about before. It must have been exciting because she stayed there for five years, right up until she came to Florida.

"Of course, her family life was nonexistent, her parents dead and that wild man brother of hers off racing stock cars somewhere. Her Thompson salary and the money her folks left her was enough so that she could afford her own apartment and she was real proud of that—said for the first time in her life she felt truly on her own.

"I don't know much about her social life there, and she'd clam up every time I asked, so I finally quit. I suspect she had a good one, though. I mean she had plenty of money, a good personality, and she is, was, so pretty. Plus, she could play a mean piano, and she loved to sing. Put that together with the flocks of bright, talented young people she must have met in New York and I'd say she had more things to do than time to do them.

"On the romance side of it, I don't know. Not a subject of conversation between us. She did say she went through the usual dating thing, the singles bars, the cocktail parties, dinner, the theater—the standard kind of stuff that I guess goes on in New York. If there was a big love in her life, I'll tell you one thing, Cam, she didn't tell me about it—not that it would have made any difference.

"When I asked her why she came to Florida, she had a variety of reasons, which may or may not have been the real answer. She said her job was getting boring, that she was starting to do the same things over and over. Said New York had lost its freshness for her, that she'd seen and done all the things she cared to. Told me the parties all seemed to run together—same people, same stories, same topics of conversation. The men seemed to sort out into two camps: attractive but married, single but dull. So she sublet her apartment and came here—temporarily, she said—to take a break, you know, get herself together and figure out what to do next. She still felt temporary about Florida when I met her, felt that way almost up to the time we got married, and then decided she'd stay. Now—now, of course, she'll never leave.

"That's what I know about Laura's life before she came here. I'm afraid it isn't an awful lot to go on."

I disagreed, told him he'd done a fine job and that I was getting a much clearer picture of her. I was getting good at the confidence-building racket, at least for an amateur. I also noted it was almost eleven o'clock, with the important part still to go. Sure, there would be time for other visits, but I was anxious to get to work quickly, and chances were whomever he came up with today would prove to be the major people in her life, and therefore the most valuable.

So, I got more coffee and blew five minutes telling him about me, just to give him a break from talking. I said I couldn't wait to hear about their life together, suggested in the interest of time that he concentrate as much as he could on providing other people I could talk to who'd been important to Laura.

"I came to Florida because I got divorced. We married too young, had kids too quickly, and it went from good to bad in a hurry, a little over five years all told. Anyway, after the divorce I just wanted to get out of Cedar Rapids, and the firm was kind enough to help by transferring me down here. Catherine's remarried since then, so I don't have that on my back, but her lawyer really stung me good on child support and that's going to be with me for a while. You know anything about divorce lawyers, Cam?"

I told him I had a more than nodding acquaintance with the breed and, as gently as I could, reminded him of the time and the need to stick to the point.

"Oh, sure, sorry, just got carried away having someone to talk to. Got to have a little background or the names won't mean anything to you.

"We'd both been in Florida for about a year when I first

met Laura. I'm older than she . . . was, by six years, from different parts of the country and different academic backgrounds and I'd been married and divorced—it's a wonder to me we ever got together at all.

"I met her at a country club dance. I wasn't a member of the club, but a friend of mine was and took me along because he said it was time I started coming out of my shell. Laura wasn't a member either; she came as the guest of the Paleys—Forrest and Elaine. That's one of the people you should talk to, Elaine Paley. Was Elaine Edwards when Laura first knew her; they were roommates at Smith their last two years. She moved in with Elaine when she came to Florida, then about nine months later, Elaine married this Forrest Paley character and left the apartment to Laura. Paley made it big in the first condominium boom and now they live in the Las Olas section of Lauderdale, as if they'd been there all their lives. She's all right, although a little too snooty for my taste; he thinks he's a financial genius instead of what he really is—a dumb contractor who got lucky. I hear she's into politics pretty good, thinking about running for alderman or the state House of Representatives or something. Anyway, she'd be worth talking to, even though we haven't seen much of them the last couple of years. Elaine Paley, Mrs. Forrest M.—they're in the book.

"Having gone through the marriage and divorce business I was pretty gun-shy about women, but Laura was pleasant to talk to and I enjoyed dancing with her. I found myself telling her all about my problems and why I'd come to Florida—all sorts of things I had no intention of telling anyone.

"The next day I called her and invited her for a pizza and the movies that Friday, no big deal, just a sort of a starter date. Well, we had a fine time, low key, no pressure, and I realized I genuinely liked being with her. So we started going out and almost a year later, I asked her to marry me. She didn't want to, at first, but I *can* be pretty persistent when it's important, and I just kept after her. She even suggested we live together, but I'm old-fashioned, I guess. I wanted to do it the traditional way. Finally, she gave in and we got married—three years and three months ago. We bought the condo in Cypress Beach and started out to live happily ever after. Never dreamed it would end this way.

"You also ought to talk to that Betty Hillson, Cam. She was Laura's best friend—at least the person closest to her. Hillson's a widow who lives directly across the court from us. We met her at the swimming pool right after we moved in. She's lonely and she likes to mother people; I thought she was a little pushy, but she and Laura hit if off right away, and they've been close ever since. So, talk to her. Even though she'll probably chew your ear off.

"Those are the only close friends I can think of. Oh, we know a lot of people—in my line you're expected to—but we weren't real big partygoers, and for whatever reason, we never seemed to get real friendly with too many people.

"I won't take too much time talking about Reverend Graham, being as you're such good friends and all; he's probably told you everything he knows by now.

"Laura thought the world of him. Spent so much time doing church things I teased her she should become a nun. I probably should have done more of it with her—might even have made some more friends or business contacts—but I'm not a church sort of person, so I never did. Reverend Graham has been a big help to me too; I'll never be able to thank him enough for it. Laura and I went through some troublesome times in our marriage, as you know. He was always there to help and I don't know what would have happened without him.

"Two other names I can think of—both first names, but getting the rest shouldn't be too hard. Dana's one of them, Dana something—he's the assistant pro at the Cypress Beach Racquet Club. The title sounds fancy, but it's really just a little place for tennis nuts. No golf course or pool or restaurant, even. Just a half dozen courts, a snack bar, and changing rooms. *We* didn't belong—I'm not that much of an athlete—but Laura did. The dues weren't that much; Laura paid for it off the interest on the money her folks left her. Said the exercise was good for her legs and what else did she have to do with her time. She played every week. I guess she was pretty good: She and this Dana guy are the club's current mixed doubles champions. I met him a couple of times and he's a very good-looking young guy—almost pretty, like an actor. Should be easy to find. The club's small and I *know* his first name is Dana.

"The only other person I can think of is a kid. About a year ago, Laura decided she wanted to teach piano. Not the usual way—with loads of children coming around. Her idea was to pick one student at a time so that she could really concentrate on bringing out individual ability. The first one was a girl Reverend Graham recommended—Katie Foster, her name was. Besides the talent, she was a cute-looking little thing; got so I used to look forward to Saturday mornings. That only lasted four months, though; her dad was transferred up north somewhere and they moved away.

"The current one is a boy named Kenny something or other—an Italian name, I think it starts with a 'D.' His schedule was Monday, Wednesday, and Friday afternoons, which was when I'd see him because we close the office early on Fridays. He's a big, awkward-looking kid. Like an overgrown puppy dog—all clumsy. You wouldn't think he'd know one end of a piano from the other, but Laura said he was talented, had made real good progress in the last five months.

"Laura wrote down all the telephone numbers she used a lot in the back of the telephone book on top of the refrigerator. If you look there I'm sure you can get Kenny's last name and his number. I'm not sure he can be much help to you, but you said anybody and everybody, so I guess you should talk to him.

"I'll try to think of some more—God knows I have plenty of time to think—but those are the ones that come to mind first.

"Oh, one other thing—Laura had an address book she kept in her desk. One of the loose-leaf kind with the alphabet tabs and all. That might be worth looking at, though she wasn't much of a letter writer."

My watch said seven minutes to noon and I knew I could count on Serkin to enforce the time limit. I closed the notebook, put it in my pocket, told Ralph what a big help he'd been, and urged him to keep on trying to remember anything and anyone that might be helpful. Just a little pep talk from the Old Coach—corny—but for now he was all we had. I didn't expect the reaction it produced.

His eyes filled up and he told me in a shaky voice that he didn't know how to thank us, that we were the only friends he had left in the world. I don't handle statements like that too well, so I just told Ralph to try to relax and remember he wasn't alone, we were all in it together.

The winner of this year's Most Treasured Clichés Award is . . . Mr. A. C. MacCardle. Tumultuous applause.

The door opened and Sergeant Serkin came in, trailed by the guard with the menacing-looking weapon. They motioned to Morgan to get up. I said good-bye and watched him leave, the guard the prescribed distance behind.

I walked with Serkin back through the labyrinth to the dayroom, talking as we went. He asked if Morgan had come up with anything useful and I said, in all honesty, that I really didn't know. I told him I had a lot of notes to sort through, which I planned to do that afternoon, and that we'd probably be in touch with Lieutenant Hampton the next day or so. I asked him to thank Hampton for the use of the room and for the coffee. In response to his question I said, yes, I did know the way out, and left.

At the end of last night's phone call, Dick had invited me to a combination dinner and status report session, but I had the afternoon to myself and I decided to invest it just as I'd told Serkin, sorting things out, or trying to, anyway.

I stopped on the way home to pick up a bucket of the Colonel's Extra Crispy, got home, changed clothes, took bucket and notebook out onto the dock, and settled in for a session of chewing and reviewing.

By the end of the afternoon, I decided we hadn't added much to the cause, at least not at first take. Maybe I'd expected too much, maybe I'd seen too many movies, maybe I wasn't very good at the job.

So far, it was a pretty slim list from which to pick a villain: a reticent stockbroker, an old school friend, a widow, an assistant tennis pro, and a piano student. Not exactly candidates for the post office wall, I thought sourly; better than nothing to go on but not *much* better.

The address book might be helpful, though, as well as the list of often-used telephone numbers. Ralph had mentioned Laura's desk. Maybe it would be worth the time to go through that desk—the whole condominium, come to think of it—in the hopes of turning up *something* more than what we had now. Suggest that to Dick tonight.

The only plus so far, from my standpoint, was that I was beginning to get a little clearer picture of both Ralph and Laura Morgan. What I saw of Laura I liked; what I saw of Ralph was less impressive. She—a tennis player, teacher of children, church worker, and kind to an old woman—sounded like an all-around nice person to know, not someone who'd earned a sash around the neck. Dick had told me Ralph was reserved. If reserved meant nonparticipative, I'd have been more inclined to agree. A curious life-style; he didn't seem to do anything other than go to work. A nice enough guy, on the basis of one meeting, but hardly Colonel Charisma.

They were relative newcomers to Florida, so they hadn't had a broad base of friends here. With no children, they couldn't use school as a means of making new contacts. So, Laura tries by getting involved with church work, but he's not "churchy"—*that* doesn't produce anything. The tennis doesn't work either, despite the fact she's obviously a good, enthusiastic player. A piano student has been coming to his house three times a week for over five months and Ralph doesn't even know the kid's last name. Easy to see why the marriage had its problems. Ralph seemed well on his way to establish the World and Olympic records for noninvolvement. No wonder she turned outside the marriage for companionship—Billy's, the old lady's, and the physical kind. Ralph evidently hadn't given her much of a choice.

About as much choice as you gave Lydia, Mr. Big Man, I thought. Where were you when The Pearl needed help? Chasing around playing a kid's game and telling war stories, that's where, Mr. Marriage Expert. If you'd been as good at spotting your own faults as you are at spotting Morgan's, maybe Lydia would still be around, which wouldn't be all bad, would it?

Oh, well, good old twenty-twenty hindsight wasn't going to solve that problem, and all these dour thoughts weren't going to be much help in finding Laura's killer, so just pack them away and go back to work, sport. Time to be on your way.

I put the luncheon debris in the garbage, took a quick shower, and changed back into Aging Ivy. Picked up the notebook, stopped along the way to buy a bottle of Château Neuf-du-Pape as a gifty, and arrived at Dick's house just after seven, still suffering from the glooms.

All of which the Ellis family dispersed in about five minutes. Susan turned out to be a vivacious, witty, brown-eyed blond from "Miz-sippi," a Chi Omega who made it easy to understand why they seem to have a lock on Miss Americas. The kids—twin girls about six who looked like Mama, and an older brother probably around ten—were energetic, friendly, and open, without being obnoxious about it.

Older brother turned out to be a football fan and a Miami Dolphins fanatic. Shortly after we'd been introduced he disappeared, then returned with a shoeboxful of trading cards, the kind kids get with bubble gum, along with warnings from ADA. He rummaged around in the box, came up with what he was looking for, and brought it over for closer inspection. What do you know? Old number eighty-eight in person, reaching out to grab an imaginary ball in one of those improbable poses the photographers always wanted.

Solemn, brown eyes looked at me respectfully. "You must have been real good, Mr. MacCardle. The card says you went to the Pro Bowl."

Well, who was I to shatter a child's illusions? I went to the Pro Bowl because the rules said each team had to have at least one representative. Hammerin' Henry, the Main Man, and I drew straws; I won. I couldn't tell him *that*, so I said something to the effect that I guess I'd done all right, but that in today's market, it would probably take six of me and a high draft choice to get him one Bob Griese card. He smiled and said he'd just hang on to what he had. Discriminating taste, rare in one so young.

Dinner was superb, particularly appreciated by one who does too much cooking for himself. Clear soup, rare roast beef, Yorkshire pudding, broccoli spears in butter, and a lovely claret to accompany them. Strawberry shortcake and espresso for dessert. I told Susan if one more thing came out of that kitchen they'd have to take me off on a stretcher.

Finally, Dick and I took brandy into his study, where I gave him a rundown on the day and what I thought of it.

Dick, bless him, disagreed: "Cam, *I* believe you did just fine for openers. These things take time and patience—don't think you can put it all together just like that! Certainly, we're short on time, woefully so, in fact. Do the best you can; that's all we can ask for. Do go talk to these people. You just never know what might turn up. I'll clear it first with Hampton, but I think you should definitely follow up on them.

"I'll also tell Hampton, if he doesn't already know it, about the telephone list and the address book. I'll ask him— can't step on toes—what his Homicide boys have done so far by way of searching the condominium and whether he thinks it makes sense for us to do more on that score.

"Meanwhile, take a break. Don't forget, it's Christmas. Speaking of which, drop by Sunday afternoon—nothing fancy, just some neighbors and a bowl of eggnog for the survivors. Unless you have a better offer, of course."

"No. That sounds good. See you around three. Please thank Mrs. Santa for the dinner. Hope you all have a fine Christmas. I know the way out."

So we said our good-byes and I went home, feeling considerably better in body and somewhat better in mind than I had on the way over.

But I couldn't shake the feeling we had a terribly long way to go without enough time to get there. Ralph's trial date had now been confirmed, according to Dick. Monday, February 15, the Honorable Hazel Flournoy presiding. We had seven weeks to try to clear Ralph Morgan, or at least give Dick grounds to request a delay.

The benefits of Susan's meal and Dick's encouragement began slipping away on the ride back, testimony to ancestry and a natural-born neuroticism. The thought of Ellis surrounded by family, gaily wrapped packages, and stockings, playing Super Daddy, should have produced good thoughts. Instead, it reminded me that my Christmas would consist of two days alone in an empty house in Lighthouse Point, remembering happier holidays past and things that might have been. Billy couldn't help, since this was the busiest of times for him, and the tube would be worse—full of children and togetherness and the nostalgia of the season. Scrooge had been right, I thought. Bah. Humbug to you, too.

The telephone was ringing as I walked in the door. In my black Scottish mood I figured there was no way that it could be good news.

Wrong, Captain Gloom. It was Pamela, she of the delicious marmalade and cantilevered swimsuit. Telling me a cancellation had stranded her for the Christmas weekend in this sordid backwoods. Wondering if there was a Colonial who could be imposed on to put her up.

Maybe it would turn out to be a Merry Christmas after all.

Ho, ho, ho.

*   *   *

I called Ellis from the wreckage of my bed, shortly after one o'clock on Sunday afternoon. Ordinarily, I'm a very quiet sleeper, so motionless that the next-day restoration chores are usually accomplished by flipping back one corner of the sheet and blanket and tucking them in. Sometime the night before a hurricane had come into my bed, a hurricane that even asleep lashed about with elbows and feet flailing like one demented.

I told Dick I was sorry I couldn't join them, but something unexpected had come up. Could I have a rain check on the eggnog? He said he understood fully, certainly I could have the rain check, and by the way, he expected an answer from Hampton Tuesday and would call as soon as he had any news. I said that sounded good and hung up the phone.

Then I turned over and told the Hurricane the next time I felt like getting kicked to death, I'd go to bed with Secretariat.

The Hurricane giggled. "Go to bed with a horse, luv? An odd lot, that thought. You'll *never* find one of your own faith. Besides, horses don't know how to do this . . . or this . . . or that. . . ."

So there went Sunday, a day customarily reserved for charitable works and thoughts.

On Monday, the Hurricane departed, leaving in her wake expressions of cheer, promises of return, and one battered survivor who, through superhuman effort, made it all the way to seven o'clock that night before turning in. Didn't move an inch, either. Not an inch.

9

Dick's telephone call caught me mid-morning Tuesday in the middle of "Wheel of Fortune," which I was watching to help me forget the pile of laundry that was overflowing the hamper in the master bathroom. When you're playing happy homemaker you just have to deal with domestic crises the best way you can. Besides, the puzzles on "Wheel of Fortune" make you concentrate on solving them, letter by letter, so it's often an educational experience. Really.

It was a long call, partly because he had a lot to say and partly because, as I'd come to learn, it takes Dick five minutes just to say hello. The gist of the call was that Lieutenant Hampton had agreed we should talk to the four people Ralph had named.

The police already had the list of telephone numbers and Laura's address book, so *that* wasn't new news to them. The telephone list didn't help much: fire and police departments, drugstore, Ralph's office, Billy (home and office), her O. B. GYN man, her dentist, the tennis club, and the piano student—whose name turned out to be Kenny DeMarco, so at least we were spared that piece of spadework. They'd called the doctors, both of whom reported that Laura was in excellent health and a conscientious keeper of regularly scheduled appointments. The DeMarco call produced the fact that Kenny DeMarco *was* taking piano lessons from her and that neither DeMarco parent had ever met Laura.

The address book suggestion turned out to be a real dud.

According to Hampton, the book was nearly new and it had a
sum total of two entries: her brother Bobby Evans and a listing for a Mrs. Nancy Baldwin of New Canaan, Connecticut.
They ran that lead down and discovered that Mrs. Baldwin
was the alumnae secretary of Laura's class at Smith. Hadn't
heard from her in over a year. Otherwise the book was blank,
as if the owner had made a conscious decision to cut off all
ties to her former life. It also served as further testimony to
the bleakness of Laura and Ralph's social life, I thought.

Dick said Hampton would allow us access to the condominium under supervision, of course, but that he, Hampton,
thought it would be a waste of time. Said a specially trained
search squad had spent two full days combing the place from
stem to stern, going through every garment in every closet,
looking under all the cushions and mattresses, rolling the rugs
back, looking in the toilet tanks and the kitchen canisters,
paging through every book and magazine. They even did the
TV cop trick of looking at the undersides of all the drawers,
in case something had been taped there.

"A typical Hampton job, Cam, slow and very, very, careful. If he says it's a waste of time, it probably is. Let's file it
under Emergency Measures for now and get on with talking
to those four people."

It seemed to me that everything we were *doing* could be
called an emergency measure, but I didn't want to put a
damper on the day, so I told Dick I'd start on it right away.

"One thing to bear in mind. This is a busy time of year
for most people, what with the long New Year's weekend and
all, so don't be disappointed if you have trouble setting up the
meetings right away."

Two hours of telephoning later, I decided that truer
words had never been spoken. I forget which of Murphy's
laws it is, but it's true—everything *does* take longer than it
should. I also discovered another Painful Truth—namely,
what was number one on my list of priorities wasn't even
close to number one for those I'd called. At least not for most
of them.

The widow lady, Mrs. Hillson, was easy—certainly she'd talk to me. Wasn't it a terrible shame and come by anytime—just give her a little time to straighten the place up.

Mrs. Forrest Paley, Laura's old roommate, was pleasant too, but unavailable, or unavailable for a while.

"Terribly sorry, Mr. MacCardle," the Eastern Establishment voice said in tones The Pearl used to call Locust Valley Lockjaw, "Forrie and I spend every New Year's in Nassau."

The very thing, I thought. Doesn't everybody?

"I'm just distraught about Laura, of course, but you've gotten me right in the middle of packing and I'm all at sixes and sevens. We will return on the tenth, which, of course, will just be too ghastly for words—unpacking, settling back in, you do understand."

Well, yeah. Sort of.

"Perhaps the morning of the twelfth would be suitable. Please call beforehand to confirm, if you don't mind. Must run now. Happy New Year. 'Bye, 'bye."

Happy New Year to you too, Lady Elaine. Do have a smashing time in Nassau. At least she hadn't said no.

Mrs. DeMarco was all suspicion. Who was I, what did I want, what had Kenny done wrong? They had already spoken to the police, told them everything they knew, and what good would upsetting poor Kenny any more do?

I answered all of her questions and suggested she call Hampton's office to prove that I was who I said I was, that the police were aware of and had approved what I was about. I suggested she call me back and gave her my number.

She called back a half hour later and grudgingly agreed to let me talk with Kenny after school tomorrow. Gave me the directions to their house in West Pompano, telling me if I frightened Kenny, she would make things very unpleasant for me.

I assured her that wasn't my intent at all and promised to be there by three.

Tracking down the tennis pro provided the only comic relief of the day. I could have simply gone over there, since it's just around the corner, but I was beginning to enjoy the telephone method, so I called.

"Cypress Beach *Racquet* Club," the female voice practically sang. "Good afternoo-on."

"Good afternoon to you. Is Dana there, please?"

"Dana Shepherd, sir?"

"How many Danas you got over there, honey?"

"Oh, my word, this *must* be Henny Youngman. We only have one Dana, Dana Shepherd, but he's off at Hilton Head until the twelfth, playing in the Trans-South Classic. Shall I take a message for him, Mr. Youngman?"

"No thanks, honey," I said, and hung up, grinning at the way she'd handled me. Henny Youngman, indeed.

I called Mrs. Hillson, and she said four o'clock would be just fine; we could have tea and a nice chat.

So there it was—a sort of a schedule—two definites, one tentative, and I could probably just drop by the Racquet Club any time after the twelfth to talk with Dana Shepherd. Not great, but the best that could be done under the circumstances, I thought.

I called Dick, gave him the details, avoided the "I told you so," hung up, and went into the kitchen to see about lunch.

10

A brass plaque on the front door said, "The Hillsons, Frank and Betty." I wondered at that, knowing she was a widow, but decided it was probably a sentimental gesture—and a nice one, at that. I pushed the doorbell, activating a miniature Big Ben inside. Somewhere around the fifth bong or sixth bing the door opened slightly, against two sets of chain locks, and the disembodied voice inside asked, "Mr. MacCardle?"

I said I was. The door closed for a moment, then swung fully wide. Betty Hillson came out, peering up at me.

"Please excuse the delay, but with all the crime around nowadays, even in this neighborhood, you just can't be too careful. Do come in please, I've tea for us and a treat, all ready."

Betty Hillson was one of those people you like at first sight. She was a short, round woman, broad-featured, with generous laugh lines punctuating both mouth and eyes, hair a cap of gray curls. A crisp white apron covered the print dress, the aqua house slippers obviously well worn and comfortable. She bustled me inside, plumped me down in a big wing chair, and went off to the kitchen, talking all the way.

"Mr. MacCardle, please call me Betty, everybody does and I won't have it any other way. Some of the young people here call me Mother Hen. They don't think I hear them, but I do and I don't resent it. Not at all. I *am* kind of a mother hen. Always have been. Now *here* we are, all nice and cozy."

She returned carrying a large silver tray, which she deposited on the butler's table. On the tray were monogrammed

linen napkins, a lovely old Limoges teapot, and two delicate
bone-white cups and saucers I was afraid to look at, let alone
handle. A butter dish, a jar of Chivers black currant pre-
serves, and what she must have been referring to as the
"treat," a plate of scones. I hadn't seen a scone since the first
and only reunion of the MacCardle clan I ever attended, but I
remembered them fondly.

"Thank you, Mrs. Hil—Betty. You can't believe how
good these look to someone named Angus Cameron MacCardle. My friends call me Cam and I wish you would, too."

So Betty and Cam it was, companions on a dreary afternoon, sitting at the fireplace sipping the Twinings and munch-
ing scones—a scene so pleasant as to almost make me forget
the purpose at hand.

"Betty, I don't think there's any way to best get at this.
I've told you who I am and what we're trying to do. The trouble is we know so little about her, or *them*, for that matter.
Ralph Morgan described you as Laura's best friend. Maybe
the easiest way to start would be if you'd tell me how you met
and just go on from there. Put in anything you think could
help us understand this whole thing better."

It was as if someone had pulled the plug at the Hoover
Dam, a solid hour of nonstop monologue. Pausing only for an
occasional sip of tea. On and on, an unbroken litany of homi-
lies, blessings, and blames. I'll have to get my brain wrung out
and pressed after this, I thought.

Finally, she ran down and stopped, like a toy whose
spring needs rewinding. "How I do go on. But I did want you
to know everything I could think of. I so hope it helps—
Laura was like a real-life daughter to me."

"Mrs.—ah—Betty, you told the police you saw Ralph
Morgan leaving his house around seven. Did you see him
come in, by any chance?"

"No, I didn't. I'm such a creature of habit. Must have my
news, local and national, then walk Muffin until it's time for
'M*A*S*H.' My very favorite program. That Alan Alda is so
cute. . . . Well, I waved to Ralph, but he looked right

through me, like I wasn't there. He can be the *strangest* person sometimes. Guess that isn't very helpful."

Very gingerly, I asked if she thought there was any chance Laura might have been seeing someone else, granted the troubles the marriage had been going through.

The easy, friendly manner evaporated and she looked at me quite coldly. "You haven't heard a word I said, young man. You ought to be ashamed of yourself. Laura was a lovely, decent person. No matter what problems they were having that simply wouldn't have occurred to her. Never in this world."

I stammered and mumbled around, finally mollifying her somewhat, but it was clear the mood was broken and the interview was over. I thanked her for the tea and scones and talk, said I hoped to see her again soon, then went home to try to condense the monologue into something useful.

And failed. There just wasn't anything to be had—other than a glowing portrait of Laura and a catalog of Ralph's shortcomings. She was an angel, an upright, God-fearing, decent, honest girl who deserved better. He was practically a hermit. Never took Laura anywhere, never wanted to do anything, to make new friends. A weak partner trying to make Heaven's Union work. And so forth, and so on.

I wrote up my notes, such as they were, put a frozen casserole in the microwave, and broke out a beer. Carried dinner into the great room, flipped on the cable television to watch hockey from Madison Square Garden.

Let's go Rangers.

I got to the DeMarco house at exactly three the next day, as I'd promised. Mrs. DeMarco met me at the screen door, looking every bit as fierce as she had sounded on the telephone.

"Please show me your driver's license, Mr. MacCardle. Do it real slow so the dog don't get overanxious."

There was a dog, too, a great big German shepherd she was holding on a choke chain—looking hopeful that Leg MacCardle was next on his diet. I eased my wallet out of the jacket pocket, fished out my license carefully, and showed it to her.

"Okay, it's you all right. Just stay where you are—be back in a minute. Let's go, Caesar."

She came back and opened the door. "Kenny isn't home yet, but he should be here pretty quick. You might as well wait inside. Maybe you can tell me what you want from Kenny."

I was just getting into it when the screen door slapped and Kenny came into the living room. He was very much as Ralph had described him, a tall, shambling kid—all arms and legs. As one of my receivers' coaches used to joke, he looked like he was going to step on his hands any minute.

"Hi, honey. This here is that Mr. MacCardle I told you about, wants to talk to you about poor Mrs. Morgan. So go ahead, Mr. MacCardle, and don't mind me. I'm staying right here every minute so you don't pull no tricky stuff on Kenny."

That wasn't exactly what I had had in mind, particularly since I wanted to ask Kenny if *he* thought Laura Morgan could have had a lover. While I was trying to find a way around that, help arrived from an unexpected source.

"Aw, *c'mon*, Ma. I'm eighteen years old, not a baby. He wants to ask questions about Mrs. Morgan fine, let him; I got nothing to hide. You know that, Ma. Now's when you always go shopping for dinner, so go. It's okay, Ma. Go on."

She started to protest, but said she did have to do some grocery shopping. She left, warning me once more not to take too much time.

"Don't mind Ma, Mr. MacCardle; she's a little over-protective, but she means well. Let's talk in my room. The living room's for best and if we go in the kitchen Caesar will take a piece of you. He hates strangers. You want a Coke?"

I nodded, and he came back with two cans clutched in an oversize paw, gesturing with the other to point the way to his room. It was a typical boy's room, pennants covering one wall, a giant poster of Farrah Fawcett on another. A single bed, overstuffed chair in a corner, student desk, and wooden chair against the far wall. Piles of athletic gear everywhere.

He motioned me to the armchair, straddled the desk

chair backward, took a big bite out of the Coke, and asked
how he could help.

I gave him pretty much the same opening I'd used with
Betty yesterday and sat back to listen.

Although the circumstances were different, as well as the
terms he used, the bottom line was like a second showing of
yesterday. She was a wonderful woman, one of the swellest
he'd ever met; a terrific teacher, patient and encouraging,
never sarcastic—treating him more like a friend than a pupil
or, worse still, a kid. On and on, all in the same vein, until
he'd used up all the superlatives.

Finally I asked him the same question that had ended my
meeting with Betty Hillson. I got a very different reaction.

"Oh, Jesus, Mr. MacCardle, how'd you find that out?
Did I leave something there? Did she write a note to me?
You can't tell Ma, okay? She'd just die, I mean she would
die. Please don't tell her, *please*, huh? I'll do anything you
want, just don't tell her."

I told him he better *start* by telling me the whole story,
from the beginning. It took him quite a while to blurt it all
out. At first it was quite innocent—she'd kissed him on the
cheek one day after he'd completed an especially difficult exercise without an error. It became a game between them: no
errors earns a kiss. Then the kisses kept getting longer and
warmer until one day she straightened up, took him by the
hand, led him upstairs, helped him undress, took off her
clothes, and brought him into her bed. It was his first experience and he was scared silly, he said. But she was patient and
gentle, told him what a man he was and how she loved to feel
him with her. Sometimes it was once a week, sometimes all
three times; one horrible week there was nothing because it
was "that time of the month."

"Been going on now for. . ."

Suddenly, things started to fit together, maybe the first
big break we'd gotten since the whole thing started. What was
it Ralph had told me? Something like ". . . the current one's

schedule is Monday, Wednesday, and Friday afternoons."
Laura had been killed on December 13. She had sexual relations sometime that afternoon. December 13 had been a Monday. A fit, a very close fit. I hoped my face wouldn't give me away while I thought what to do next.

I realized the boy was still talking.

"It's really scary when you stop to think about it, isn't it?"

"Isn't what scary?"

"What I just told you. Geez, weren't you listening?"

"Sorry, Kenny, I was thinking about something else. Try me again."

"What I said was if it had been any other week I'd a been there the day she was killed. I mean it was a Monday and all. But that was the week of the Sunshine State Basketball Invitational up in Jax. We did pretty good—won on Saturday and Sunday, got beat in the semis Monday night. Otherwise I'd a been there—sure as hell. Please don't tell Ma, Mr. MacCardle. Promise?"

I promised, thanked him for all his help, asked him to call me if he thought of anything more, and left.

Beat my hand half to death on the steering wheel going home. Dammit. Just when things looked as if they were starting to gel—poof—the magician's wand waves and back we go to square one. Dammit. Enough to drive a grown man to drink.

Which was exactly what I proposed to Billy right after I got home. Take off the collar, come with me, and we'll get really bent—bring in what had better be a more productive New Year. Nothing to do until Madam Queen returns next week from Nassau. Just go out and really tear it up, put a lousy year out of its misery.

Billy said he'd been invited to five or six parties by his parishioners and that he really had to go—at least for a while. He urged me to come along, saying that this way I'd have a fighting chance of *surviving* into the New Year.

In the end I went with him, had a marvelous time, and woke up the next morning feeling only slightly subhuman.

Virtue is its own reward.

11

A telephone call to Mrs. Paley Monday afternoon produced that incredible accent, an invitation for "elevenses" next day, and directions on getting there. Even the address sounded formidable: 1410 Royal Palm Way, Las Olas. Very old money. On one's best behavior, old boy, top of the form, mustn't let the side down. But what in the world were "elevenses"?

The house was stunning, rambling, single-story, Spanish motif. Tiles, arches, fountains, hanging plants—all simple, tailored, understated elegance. A butler answered the soft chime. An-honest-to-God, right-off-the-set butler, complete with stiff upper lip. Took my name, told me Mrs. Paley was expecting me, and that I was to wait by the pool. Escorted me through the cool, dark house out to an enormous screen-enclosed pool overlooking a canal, pointed to a rust-colored couch almost as big as the *Lexington*, and bowed his way out. Helluva a way to spend a Tuesday morning, I thought, hoping I didn't look as out of place as I felt.

Elaine Paley was equally stunning. A tall woman—I guessed around five feet nine—in lime green espadrilles that matched the silk blouse tucked into off-white linen slacks. Fair-complexioned, with outsize sunglasses perched on a sheaf of honey-colored hair. High cheekbones, delicate nose, firm chin, a pale shade of lipstick, sparingly applied. An Elaine, all right—not an El, and never, never an Ellie, I thought, feeling more than ever like a Bedouin at a B'nai B'rith dinner.

She strode across the pool deck, ramrod straight, without the slouch tall women often effect, the butler with a large wheeled cart trailing in her wake. She introduced herself with a firm handshake, took a seat on the couch, and motioned the butler to open the cart's cover.

"Elevenses" turned out to be a choice of assorted juices, croissants, coffee, and booze, or any combination thereof. Mrs. Paley ordered guava juice, croissant, and coffee. I opted for a tall glass of tomato juice, not daring to even think about juggling all that crockery in my lap. She dismissed the butler, telling him to stay on call should anything more be needed. Large, hazel eyes looked me over carefully, and evidently decided I seemed reasonably harmless and wasn't likely to make off with the silver.

"I think we can do away with the Mrs. Paley, Mr. Mac-Cardle routine. Cam, you said—that's an odd name. Still, in Nassau, I'm known as Pookie. It's a hangover from the Smith days and a name I hope never reaches the mainland. Cam and Elaine, then. Right?"

Talk about icebreakers. I couldn't imagine a creature like that ever being called Pookie by *anyone*, and I told her that, feeling more comfortable by the minute as we chatted. Gone were the Locust Valley Lockjaw and the grande dame manner of the telephone person. The real-life version was warm, down to earth, and clearly well suited for politics.

"You owe me one, Cam. I saw you go fifty-seven yards in the Orange Bowl to beat the Dolphins *and* the spread. Cost me a very expensive dinner at Jimmy's."

Then, on a much more sober plane: "You can imagine how I feel about Laura. I'll do anything I can to help. It was a dirty, savage way for anyone to die, let alone someone I've known and loved since we were practically children."

I asked her to start with college and go from there, got the little notebook out of my pocket, sat back, and listened.

They had become friends their sophomore year at Smith, both dating boys who were Dekes at Amherst. Found they had similar interests and lots in common, including roommates they didn't particularly like. Decided to room together junior year, and it worked out so well they continued through to graduation. They exchanged dates, advice, and Christmas presents. They studied together, partied together, spent alternate vacations at each other's house. When Laura's parents were killed, Elaine had driven her home, helped her through the service and the estate settling, convinced her to go back and finish college. A close, caring relationship, in many ways similar to Billy's and mine, I thought.

After graduation they went their separate ways—out of necessity, not out of choice, Elaine said. Laura had to work and wanted to, going into advertising after a brief vacation. Elaine went home to Florida to live a life of dedicated decadence, as she put it: golf, sailing, dances, parties, with enough Junior League volunteer work to make her feel marginally respectable.

Granted the distance, they stayed in reasonably close touch over the years—regular letters, once-a-month phone calls, Christmas cards, and gifts. Laura spent one week a winter with her and convinced Elaine to spend two weeks one fall in New York.

Then Elaine got a call from her one night around two o'clock, sounding despondent, depressed, almost suicidal. Said she didn't know what to do with her life anymore, didn't really care, crying openly over the phone. Elaine spent over two hours with her, calming her down, talking it through, urging her to close the apartment in New York, get a leave of absence from her job, and come to Florida for a rest.

All of which Laura did, arriving in Florida looking like a basket case, Elaine said, pallid face, shaking hands, jumpy as a cat.

"You never knew her. She looked a lot like the singer Claudine Longet, pretty but projecting an air of vulnerability. People just wanted to put an arm around her and say, 'It'll be all right, now. I'll protect you from the slings and arrows.' Well, when she got off the plane, she made Claudine Longet look like a model for Assertiveness Training."

Elaine said she just about had to rebuild the girl from scratch, physically, emotionally, and socially. She didn't probe into what had happened, thinking Laura wasn't strong enough to handle it—that she'd talk about it when she was ready. Good food, good weather, and Elaine's circle of friends were a big help, and gradually Laura began to come around. The Party Season was going full blast, from Key West to Palm Beach, with more invitations than any one person could deal with, and soon the restoration job was completed.

"Then I married Forrie and Laura and I started drifting apart, though I didn't mean for it to happen. I gave up my share of the apartment and we went on a six-month round-the-world honeymoon while Forrie's men built this house.

"I called her right after we got back, had her over for dinners and swims, brought her to a couple of dances at the club, but it wasn't the same—guess it never is after you get married.

"Then she took up with that dreary little man. I never could understand what she saw in Ralph Morgan and I tried to talk some sense into her, tactfully, but Laura wasn't having any of it. She said he had 'hidden' qualities. Perhaps he does, but the operative word is '*hidden*.' The man is terminally shy. When she married him, I stood up with her in front of the judge. Believe me, I wasn't crying because I thought the wedding was beautiful.

"They moved into a tacky condominium in Cypress Beach. We went there once for dinner and it was so strained Forrie swore never again. So there she was, up in Cypress Beach, married to a man Forrie and I both feel uncomfortable with. What could I say? 'Come, but please tell Ralph it's all right if he speaks!' Easier to do nothing, which, I'm afraid, is what I've done.

"About two years ago, I got involved in politics. Now some people want me to run for the state House of Representatives, so it's become a full-time job. I think I'm too silk stocking a candidate, but you never know. I mean, look at John Lindsay and the Kennedys.

"I feel responsible for her . . . and I always will; she came to Florida because of me. Whatever help you think I can be, all you have to do is ask."

I thanked her, told her how much I'd enjoyed meeting her and that perhaps I could buy her and her husband a dinner to pay off my debt.

She smiled and walked me out to the car, waving as I pulled away.

Her history, while interesting, really hadn't added much, but she was a most impressive lady, very different from what I'd expected. I could understand why she and Laura had been so close and why helping Laura was important to her.

I wondered what had happened that made Laura come apart in New York. I doubted we'd ever find out, if our progress so far was any indicator. The trial was a month away and we had zippo.

Sour thoughts—a poor ending for an otherwise sterling day.

12

A hard, flat wind from the north had blown in overnight, dropping the temperature, keeping the snowbirds off the beaches, and scaring hell out of the orange growers. Smudge pots tonight, I thought, remembering looking down during a night flight onto a scene from Dante's *Inferno*, half of Florida seemingly ablaze.

Pushed by the wind, the sign swung gently on its gimbals, attracting my attention. ENTRANCE it proclaimed in Old English, CYPRESS BEACH RACQUET CLUB. MEMBERS ONLY. It was built on a cul-de-sac, tennis courts on either side of a two-lane road, widening into a turnaround dominated by a low, curving clubhouse with a flagstone terrace and a double, French-door entry in the middle of the building.

I parked where the little arrow told me to, picked up the notebook, and walked up the flagstone steps into the clubhouse. It was divided functionally in thirds, men's lockers to the left, ladies' to the right, the center mainly devoted to a lounging area. In the rear was a white, louvered double door, the sign above it indicating the location of the snack bar and the office—which was where I headed.

The office was just barely big enough to warrant the name, consisting mostly of a wide, waist-high counter running wall to wall, and behind it, a standard-issue, tan-colored metal desk and stenographer's chair, which took up the balance of the space.

The woman who sat at the desk, pounding away on a

106

battered Olivetti and muttering to herself, was definitely *not* standard issue. On a scale of one to ten, this one's a fifteen, I thought, ponytail and all. A ponytail is the acid test for great facial characteristics—only those with superb cheekbones, jaw, and ears can pull it off successfully.

The telephone on the counter rang. As she jumped up to answer, it became apparent that bounteous Mother Nature hadn't stopped with the face—the burnt orange tanktop accenting what Lydia used to call "healthy upper frontals."

"Cypress Beach Racquet Club. Good mo-oorning."

Well, what do you know? As Mel Allen used to say, "How *about* that, Yankee fans."

She hung up, saying she was sorry for the delay. Said it was time to send out delinquent bill notices, a job she hated. What could she do for me, Mr. ah . . .

"Youngman. Henny Youngman."

"*You're* the one. Look, I'm really sorry about that, sir. Don't know what came over . . . Why are you laughing?"

"Because I thought it was pretty funny. Besides, you ought to see yourself babbling around trying to apologize. That's a pretty spectacular blush."

"It only comes on when I'm making an idiot of myself, like now. I'm Carole Cummings, and if I remember right, you were looking for Dana Shepherd, correct?"

"Correct, Carole Cummings. I was and still am. My name's MacCardle, Cam MacCardle—unless you like Henny better."

"Dana's here, Mr. MacCardle. Should be on court six with Mr. Waterman, according to the sign-up board. Want to wait here?"

"It's Cam, Carole, and no, I think I'll just walk down there. Thanks for your help, wouldn't want to take you away from the delinquent notices."

Pretending not to notice the tongue she stuck out at me, I wandered over to the court, sat on the middle tier of a three-level bleacher thing, and watched the last ten minutes of the lesson.

Mr. Waterman had everything you need to play top-flight tennis—except talent. He had the oversize Prince racquet, Adidas tennis shoes, and a coordinated Fila outfit—oyster-white with orange stripes—that clashed violently with his over-red face. His strokes reminded me of the old joke about Buddy Hackett's golf swing—it really did look as if he were fighting off a swarm of bees.

Young Shepherd was remarkably patient with him, standing at the net beside a huge box of tennis balls, feeding soft shots to Mr. Waterman's backhand and forehand, pretending not to notice as the fat man hit returns into the net and, occasionally, over the wall.

Finally, mercifully, the exhibition concluded. Shepherd said some encouraging words about remarkable improvement, the frightening magenta color began to disappear from Mr. Waterman's face, and he clomped off to the showers. You're safe for another year, Bjorn, I thought, no matter how remarkable the improvement rate.

I got up, walked over to Shepherd, and introduced myself. Told him what I was doing and how I'd gotten his name. Asked him if he had time to talk today or would some other time be more convenient.

He said he hadn't another lesson until two, suggested we get in out of the wind, pick up sandwiches at the snack bar, and talk in the men's locker room. All of which made sense to me. I suddenly realized I was shivering. Thin blood.

Up close, Shepherd was smaller than he'd seemed on the court—about five-seven I guessed, the bantam rooster size all the good ones seemed to be these days. The sun had bleached his blond hair nearly white, setting off the heavy tan that only people who make their living outdoors acquire. Ralph's description of him as "movie-star handsome" had been right—light blue eyes framed by long, golden eyelashes, blinding white teeth, an almost petulant mouth with the nowadays requisite mustache. This guy must be a killer with the groupies, I thought. Wonder how he gets time to play tennis. He walked with a controlled, almost-feline grace, toed-in, on the balls of his feet, each movement precise.

Over lunch he told me his background—pretty standard, he guessed. Born in La Jolla, practically grew up with a racquet in his hand. Junior's champion, high school all-American, scholarship to USC. Good enough for the little tournaments, but not good enough for the WCT tour, Wimbledon, or Flushing Meadows. Winters here, summers at a club in Long Island, both chosen because they provided grocery money and sufficient time flexibility to go on competing, waiting for the big break.

It was a depressing story, I thought. The determination, the endless hours of practice, the early successes, and the hope—now reduced to hitting pit-a-pat shots to kids and fat men at a third-rate tennis club. Dreams die hard.

I swung the conversation back to Laura Morgan, how they'd met, what he thought of her, anything else he felt might be of help.

"Well, of course, I was simply devasted by the news. We all were, but I was especially. I mean, I just wept. I didn't go to the memorial service; it would have been too much to bear."

He went on to tell me she was one of the most active members when he'd come to the club two years before—in the middle of the "A" ladders for singles, doubles, and mixed doubles. He watched her play, saw that her serve was the big flaw in an otherwise solid game, had given her serving lessons and marveled at her improvement, not at all like the fat, old foofs and the horrible little children he usually had to suffer.

"Besides the tennis, she was so marvelously simpatico. Not at all like those rich bitches who came to show off their outfits and play My Husband Is A Louse. She was an absolute angel to the staff. I mean, an *angel*."

They better not give this guy a loyalty oath, I thought, or he's long gone. He might well be right about the members, but I was sure they weren't ready for that kind of character analysis. As he talked, I began to have some disquieting notions about Dana Shepherd. Maybe the mouth, the walk, the almost-dainty way he nibbled at his chicken salad, the words, the inflections, all of it combined. I wondered if the theory of Bored Wife and Handsome Tennis Pro was about to go up the flue, along with all the rest.

His response to my question on the possible identity of Laura's extracurricular partner settled that issue once and for all.

"Mr. MacCardle, what the members do with their private lives is their business, no matter how lurid. I *adored* Laura Morgan, but not *that* way; surely you're perceptive enough to understand."

Surely, I was. No groupies for Dana. Not now, not ever. Good-bye, theory. Hello, dead end. You're getting to be a constant companion.

I was thanking Dana and getting ready to leave when it hit me. Something so simple, I wondered why I hadn't thought of it right away. We were sitting in the men's locker room. There were lockers for women on the other side of the building. Laura had been a member for at least two years. Wasn't it logical to suppose she had a place to store her tennis gear? What if she did, lummox? What'll that prove? Only one way to find out.

We walked over to the office, Carole dug around in the file drawer and came up with a mimeographed sheet. They did have an entry: Morgan, Mrs. Laura E., locker thirty-six. Carole said, quite properly, she didn't feel right about somebody nonfamily cleaning out the locker. I gave her Lieutenant Hampton's telephone number and suggested she call over there for permission.

"I guess it's okay. There probably aren't any secret plans for building atom bombs in there. I'll go with you to make sure the coast is clear and keep the ladies out. Dana, please cover for me. Won't be gone long."

She came out of the locker room indicating there was no

one inside, said she'd stand guard there, and could I please make it snappy.

True to form, I'd forgotten to ask for the combination. Went back outside, took the deserved ribbing, wrote down the combination: 15 right, 9 left, 25 right.

Got the door open on the first try, feeling like Willy Sutton. All the usual stuff was there; a Head Pro Model racquet hung cased on the inside of the locker door. On the locker bottom an empty blue-and-white Lands' End tennis bag, the monogram LEM worked into the sailcloth. Next to it, a scruffed pair of Tretorn tennis shoes and two pairs of sockettes, with the little balls at the backs. On hangers—a blouse, skirt, and cardigan sweater, in matching blue and white, all with the LEM monogram.

What were you expecting? I wondered, folding all the clothing into the tennis bag—ordinary, all ordinary. Started clearing out the top shelf—sun visor, stacked underwear, sunglasses, can of deodorant spray—and found something very unordinary buried underneath—a flat manila envelope eight-and-a-half-by-eleven, with a metal-tab closure.

Even I know manila envelopes are not standard-issue tennis gear, so I stuffed it into the little canvas bag, double-checked to make sure the locker was empty, swung the door closed, and walked out.

"No atomic bomb secrets?" Carole asked.

"'Fraid not, just the usual gear. Not even microfilm."

"Figures, she didn't look too dangerous."

"If Henny calls sometime, would you let him buy you a drink?"

"You clod"—laughing—"try me. 'Bye, Cam."

"'Bye, Carole."

I could hardly wait to get to the car. Put it down to intuition, to all the frustrations we'd had, to being naturally nosy, but I had to know what was in that envelope. Now.

I opened the car door, threw the tennis bag onto the front seat, jumped in beside it, closed the door. Rummaged around in the bag, fished out the envelope, pushed the metal tabs up, opened it.

There were three things in the envelope: two letters, which I scanned quickly, and found intriguing and rather self-explanatory, plus a savings account passbook from the Chase Manhattan Bank of New York—which made no sense at all to *me*, but might to someone who knew what they were doing.

Got to get Ellis involved, I thought. Quick. I drove home, carried the bag and envelope in, and left them on the table in the foyer. Telephoned Dick, who wasn't there but was expected back around four and could she take a message, sir?

You could. You for sure could. Please ask him to stop at Mr. McCardle's on the way home. If that wasn't convenient, make sure he telephoned Mr. MacCardle tonight. Gave her the number.

I broke out a self-congratulatory beer, carried it and the envelope over to the breakfast booth. Sat rereading the letters and trying to make more sense of the passbook—waiting for Ellis. A half-forgotten piece from a Winston Churchill speech surfaced as I thought. As the war had begun to turn in Britain's favor, he'd said, "This is not the end. It is not even the beginning of the end. But it is, perhaps, the end of the beginning."

My sentiments exactly. Let's hear it for history majors.

14

The first letter was handwritten on corporate stationery, the logotype J.WALTER THOMPSON dominating the top of the page. In the left-hand margin, in smaller type, R. PHILLIP CORWIN, and a title underneath the name, *Senior Vice-President*. It had been written a little over ten years ago. The script was open, Palmer Method, each line running straight across the page.

My Dearest Laura,

I realize this comes to you in a moment of great sorrow. I also realize that it may shock and confuse you. Please be patient and try to understand.

To you I have always been "Uncle Phil," your godfather and your parents' close friend. That is not the whole truth, but I could not tell you until this moment.

I am your father. You are my daughter, Laura, my only child, and I love you very much.

It has been an agony for me, watching you grow up, taking such pride in you and all you have done, and not being able to share that pride with you or anyone but your mother.

With Helen gone—God rest her soul—only two people in all the world know—you and I. Jim was never aware of it and now he never will be.

-continued overleaf-

I turned the letter over, thinking what an incredible blow it must have been to her. The uniform script marched on:

113

-2-

Please don't blame Helen; she was a good woman and a loving mother. Human beings are frail creatures, and she and I are no exceptions.

There were problems in their marriage two years after Bobby was born. Your mother felt isolated, penned in, locked away in a world of household drudgery. Nowadays we probably would label it an identity crisis.

I introduced your parents to each other when Jim and I were at Harvard and Helen at Wellesley. I was best man at their wedding. In her need, Helen turned to me for comfort. Comfort became love and love produced you.

We couldn't tell Jim then or ever. The knowledge would have crushed him. Divorce was much more a moral stigma in those days, for parents and children as well.

I agreed to go through the bittersweet charade of being your godfather, your "Uncle Phil." It's why I never married. The three people I loved most in life belonged to one another and I dared not change that.

I am enclosing a cashier's check for ten thousand dollars, which should see you through until your inheritance clears the probate process; if not, you have only to call.

When you graduate from Smith, I want you to come to see me here. We can talk about what you want to do for a living and you know I will help in any way possible.

I close this letter, dearest daughter, with the joy that I can finally call you that.

I ask only that you accept me for what I am, your devoted father.

The poor son of a bitch. Twenty-plus years of keeping a secret that would have blown his best friend's world apart. Of having to playact on weekend visits and parties with the only woman he ever loved. Of treating the flesh of his flesh as a normal godfather would, while aching to hold her close and tell her what she meant to him. What it must have cost him— but he'd honored the agreement until he no longer had to.

What a hard letter it must have been to write. I thought it was a very good job, granted the circumstances, the between-the-lines pictures emerging more strongly than the written words. I hoped Laura had been mature enough to get those pictures, that she had come through the shock of it without hating either one of them. Youth is not a time of great understanding, more a binary world of yes-no, off-on, black-white. I found myself vicariously urging Laura to find the strength to understand, to reach out for the writer, who so clearly loved her. Yessir, some letter indeed.

The other letter was quite different. It was written five years after her father's, in a hard-to-read, crabbed scrawl on beige stationery with the writer's name and address at the top.

Bryant W. Melton III
219 East 65th Street
New York, New York 10021

It was a much shorter letter, but it's meaning was equally clear.

Dear Laura,

I haven't answered your telephone calls because I wanted to avoid another nasty scene—this is an easier way for me. Besides, talking won't do us any good; we always wind up saying the same things over and over.

I'm not going to divorce Sarah—I can't and I find I don't want to. She and the children haven't done anything to deserve it. It's all been my fault—my fault and yours.

I'm glad you agree about the abortion. It's really the cleanest way in the long run. I'm told the clinic is completely sanitary and painless—the whole thing only takes a weekend. Please be sure to send me the bill when you get it.

I think it would be best for both of us if we didn't see each other or try to communicate. Let us just recognize it is over and treat it like two adults, not as if we were the only people in the world who ever went through this. As your Italian friend says, *Que sera, sera* —only in our case we just weren't meant to be.

I know you will come through all right, and I wish you
nothing but good thoughts.

Sincerely,
Bryant

Sincerely? My Great-Aunt Fannie, I thought. If ever a
five-star bastard was born, this guy was the model. I was as
mad at him as I'd been sorry for her father, and I wondered
how letters from strangers could produce such reactions in
me—getting too involved with the whole thing, I supposed.

But what a letter—particularly in light of the subject. I
could visualize Laura reading it—alone, pregnant, scared half
to death, needing help and assurance and love. Then getting
kicked right in the teeth by the sanctimonious ass who'd gotten her into the whole mess. How had she reacted? What had
she done, her world pulled down around her ears in sham-
bles?

And *Que sera, sera* —great galloping Jesus! You're getting emotional, MacCardle.

Damn right.

I tossed the letters aside and picked up the savings account passbook. It had been opened with an initial deposit of
$10,000 ten years ago, showing an additional deposit of
$42,350 a year later. There was a record of steady with-
drawals, plus interest accumulated, over the next four years.
Then a big withdrawal of $15,000. A three-year period of zero
activity followed, the book indicating only the payment of
quarterly interest to the holder, the principal balance fluctuat-
ing in the $10,000 to $11,000 range. A little more than a year
ago, according to the book, the account began receiving deposits. Always the same amount—a thousand dollars—and
always in the first ten days of the month. Every month, right
up through this December.

I was beginning to make some sense of it when the doorbell rang. It was Dick Ellis; evidently My Lady of the Switch-
board had gotten through to him. I brought him in, unshod
him, got two beers, brought them and him back to the breakfast area.

I sat him down and gave him a capsule of the day—Carole, Mr. Waterman, Dear Dana, and all. Told him about my hunch, showed him the results. I asked him to read the letters while I continued to puzzle over the bankbook, said we'd work on it together when he was finished. He didn't take very long with the letters.

"Dammit, this really looks great. What the hell made you think of a locker?"

"I'd like to credit sheer genius, Counselor, but it's more equal parts of desperation and good luck."

"Never mind. It's the first solid stuff we've turned up yet. Well done, m'boy. What do you make of the bankbook?"

"Take a look at it and then I'll tell you—see if you agree. Part of it still has me stumped, though. By the way, nobody knows about these, unless Ralph does."

The horn-rimmed glasses came out along with the pipe, as he gave the book a closer look. He finished, laid aside the glasses, and pushed the book over to me. I told him what I thought, trying to balance the dates and activities shown with the bits and pieces of information I'd gathered.

"This is all guesswork, but I think it hangs together—at least up to a point. We can assume the ten-thousand starting deposit was the check she got from her real father. The next big chunk—the odd-lot one—is probably what her folks left her after taxes and greedy lawyers got done with it. As I recall, it takes about a year for an estate to clear probate."

"Near enough. Greedy lawyers, indeed."

"Thought you'd like that. The period of withdrawals coincides pretty closely to the time she spent in New York. She told Ralph she had her own apartment, didn't split it like so many career gals do. That's expensive—believe me, I know. Advertising agencies don't pay well, at least not for beginners. Lydia told me she went to an agency interview her last year at Columbia and laughed at them when they told her what the salary was—and she was an MBA. So I would guess the withdrawals, plus whatever Laura was getting paid, allowed her the apartment and her living expenses.

"The big withdrawal is a little spookier, but there may be an answer for it. Elaine Paley convinced her to come to Florida to pull herself back together. The timing looks just about right. She had to have some money to live on; a friend's generosity goes just so far. She probably figured if things didn't work out down here she could always put the rest of the money back in the bank.

"Things did work out, though—in a fashion—and the no-withdrawal period starts roughly around the time she got married. We know from the financial review Hampton's people did that they weren't exactly Mr. and Mrs. Gotrocks. On the other hand, Ralph did well enough so they could live without using any of her money because we know they were even building a little in the bank here."

"Once she was settled, though, why didn't she shut down the New York account?"

"I don't know—maybe sentiment, maybe something else. I just don't have anything solid to go on. Ralph said she was independent, told me she wasn't committed to Florida in the beginning. Maybe she kept it for getaway money, but I'm really guessing now. The real mystery to me is the deposits. We know she started giving piano lessons around then, but a thousand bucks a month will buy one helluva lot of piano lessons. It can't be that. Must be something else. But what? Beats me, Chief."

"Beats me too, but I know three things: One, we're not going to figure it out whacking around at it tonight. Besides, you've had a long and—let me add—most promising day. Two, that's the kind of thinking Hampton and his people get paid to do. I'll try to set up something with him tomorrow afternoon. Stick tight, the office will call you. Three, Ralph may be able to help. I'll talk to him tomorrow morning.

"Meanwhile, its off to Susan and the troops. Get a good night's sleep. You earned it."

I saw him out, whipped up a pot of Dinty Moore's beef

stew—bachelor's delight—washed it down with most of a jug of Chianti, cleaned up, and turned in, mind still churning.

My explanation of her financial activity seemed plausible, seemed to fit with what we knew. All except the deposits. What in the world were they all about? I wondered, as I went to sleep. What could they possibly be?

15

"Blackmail," Lieutenant Hampton said, looking across his desk at us. "Extortion is what those deposits could possibly be. They do fit the standard pattern—same amounts of money, regular schedule, an out-of-state bank. Still, the people you've talked to so far don't seem the likeliest of prospects, MacCardle."

"We never even thought of blackmail, Lieutenant. Wouldn't *that* be something? If it is, then we'd have a real solid reason why Laura was killed. And you're right, it would explain the deposits."

"Don't go off the deep end. It's only one possible explanation."

"But a good one, Lieutenant. Assume for a minute it *is* blackmail. I agree we can throw out the kid and old Mrs. Hillson. That still leaves Dana Shepherd—though he's not exactly a closet case—and Mrs. Paley. She and Laura go back a long way."

"You're stretching. A two-bit tennis pro? A political candidate with Moral Majority backing? Come on. If it is extortion—and that's a mighty big 'if'—your New York letter writers look far more promising. Particularly Mr. Melton; God knows he apparently provided more than sufficient cause."

"What about my client, Wade?"

"What about him, Mr. Ellis? Look, MacCardle did a nice piece of police work, coming up with that envelope. Some people I know are going to take a little chewin' for it. But what does it prove? Maybe extortion, maybe not.

"You know as well as I do it doesn't alter the basic facts in any material manner. Morgan still cannot prove any part of his story. Everything that was pointing to him as the prime suspect still does. So, Mr. Morgan stays put."

"But don't you agree the blackmail angle is worth pursuing, Lieutenant?"

"Yes, I do, even though I think it's a long shot. I can't justify putting anyone on it full time, but I will have somebody run a check on all four of the local bank statements. Maybe something will pop. Meanwhile, MacCardle can go talk to those two people in New York. Come up with something solid and we'll have another look. Otherwise, status quo.

"Again, Mr. MacCardle, a nice piece of work. Stay in touch, sing out if you need help. Good afternoon, gentlemen."

We went back to the Pelican's Roost for some sustenance and breathing room. Extortion seemed to make more and more sense as we talked. My favorite target was Bryant Melton III. After all, I argued, they say hell hath no fury like a woman scorned, and she'd been scorned, all right. Surely the clinic kept records on all their patients. It wouldn't be very hard to get hold of good old Bry and ask him if the wife and kiddies wouldn't be interested to know there'd almost been an addition to the family. Sincerely *yours*, Sugar.

Dick agreed, but said we shouldn't dismiss Phillip Corwin out of hand. Yes, he'd promised in the letter she could have money anytime she asked. But, we didn't know Laura's reaction to the letter or what the nature of their relationship had been while she was in New York. It could have gone sour. Not likely, but worth talking about . . . as long as I was in the neighborhood.

"One other thing. I visited with Ralph Morgan this morning. Total shock. He knew about the bank account, but he thought she'd closed it long ago. He told her to right after they got married, and she said she would. Strike one.

"The ex-lover was a blow. Laura never mentioned either the man or the abortion. Finally said, what the hell, he'd been married before too; this was sort of the same thing. Strike two.

"The true father thing really got to him. Not the fact of it, but that Laura never told him about it. I'm afraid he's beginning to discover there may have been lots of things Laura never told him. Strike three and out, Mr. Morgan."

"Did you ask him about Laura's giddy afternoon adventure?"

"You must be joking. He's had about all he can stand, and I'll bet you that one would draw a blank too."

"Probably, but I'd still give a pretty penny to know who it was. You want a final, final drink?"

"No, thanks, I've got to get back to the office and you have some logistics problems to juggle. Don't forget to keep all your receipts; I've got a very fussy bookkeeper."

"Logistics problems" weren't the right words. "Nightmare" would have been a better choice. Scheduling two appointments and getting airline passage to fit without a long layover in New York was one further proof of Murphy's other law: Everything is harder than it looks.

I couldn't get to see Bryant Melton until Friday, the twenty-second. He'd been most suspicious—almost hostile—when I mentioned Laura Evans. Wanted to know if I was with the police, mumbled something about it all being ancient history, better dead and buried—a choice of words that made me wince.

I assured him I wasn't any kind of police, that Laura had hired me to track down a mutual friend of theirs. I said I couldn't mention the name on the phone because Laura felt that said mutual friend might vanish if forewarned.

Just as I felt Mr. Melton might vanish if he knew why I *really* wanted to see him. A thin story, but he bought it and agreed to meet me at the Yale Club, in the Men's Bar at one. I said I knew where it was, thanked him, and hung up.

Phillip Corwin was harder, principally because he was out of the country. His superefficient secretary sounded more like a travel agent. Mr. Corwin was presently in the Rome office, would be with the Paris and London branches next week, flying home Sunday, the twenty-fourth, on the Concorde. Monday would be impossible, of course, first day back and whatnot. Tuesday at two looked free. Would I please call early morning to confirm and could she tell Mr. Corwin what this concerned?

I would and she could. I told her it had to do with a friend of Mr. Corwin's named Laura Evans and said I was sure Mr. Corwin would be most interested and receptive to seeing me. Two down.

The airline situation was the worst of all. I had forgotten how hard it is to get in and out of Florida during the Season. Dick had agreed to my flying first class, since, as he put it, my expenses to date hadn't made that much of a dent in the exchequer. First class didn't help. Tried all the combinations— Miami, Fort Lauderdale, West Palm, even looked at going through Washington to pick up the shuttle. Nothing, booked solid; standby might work, but they weren't making any promises. Just as I was beginning to feel like the last refugee out of Shanghai, the nice Eastern Airlines lady called to say she could get me on an Airbus leaving Lauderdale at 9:15 Wednesday night, arriving LaGuardia at 11:47. I grabbed it.

I made hotel reservations at the Barclay. The location was handy to both my meetings, and there was an atmosphere about the Barclay I'd always liked. It doesn't have the flash of the Hilton or the new Hyatt, but it's a comfortable, almost Old World kind of hotel. The Pearl and I had stayed there once when the apartment was being painted, and fell in love with it.

Midweek, I had a minor inspiration—I called Elaine

Paley and asked her if the name Bryant Melton meant any-thing to her.

"Melton, Bryant Melton, yes, I think that does sound vaguely familiar, but why? No . . . don't interrupt. Let me think. Ah, got it. One night, long after she came down, Laura looked particularly happy. She said she guessed she was over Bryant Melton for good. I asked her who that was and she said he was an old New York flame that had finally fizzled out. That was it. Why, Cam?"

"The police found an old letter from him in Laura's things. Pretty much what you just said; thought I'd ask, though. As long as I have you, can you think of any other New York Laura contacts? Anybody you might have met on your vacation there?"

"Ah, no, it was so long ago and there were just scads of people. Nobody I'd care to remember though, sorry."

"No problem, Elaine, thanks again. Good-bye now."

"'Bye, Cam."

As I said, a minor inspiration.

I had the winter clothes pressed, hung them in the gar-ment bag, got out the overcoat, and shut off the newspaper temporarily—no sense advertising you're away. Dropped the car in the long-term parking lot, checked in, waited for them to board first class.

The Airbus was chockablock, the roar from the back guaranteeing the stews were in for a long flight north. My seatmate turned out to be a very pretty girl with a T-shirt that read, "I Got It At Arthur's." She turned to me, yawned, and said, "Mister, I'm just flat bushed from all the partyin'. Going to sleep all the way to New York. That suit you?"

Suited me fine. In fact, somewhere around Jacksonville, I joined her.

16

New York in January is not my favorite place. When The Pearl and I had lived there we always tried to get away in January, even if it meant going to Charlotte. The city is magnificent in April and October, bearable for the balance of the year, but the pits in January. Ask anyone who lives there.

The wind from the East River bit through my topcoat as I hurried down Park Avenue through a midday made dark by overcast and occasional snow flurries. The lunch-hour strollers —so much a part of the street scene in other months—were nowhere to be seen, driven indoors by the bleakness of the day and the numbing cold. Only those like me—people whose meetings or errands couldn't wait—were out, all of us moving along briskly to cut the discomfort as much as possible, trying to keep the blood circulating.

I walked through the lobby of the Pan Am Building, the long way to get where I was going, but I needed a break from the cold. Riding the long escalator down to the nearly deserted floor of Grand Central Station, I looked to the left and saw the giant Kodak transparency that dominates that end of the esplanade. Sure enough, there were Mommy and Daddy and two little kiddies, all in bathing suits, romping in the sun and surf—having a wonderful time, "glad we're here and you're there." I hope you all get sunburned, I thought uncharitably, cursing the twisted mind of the oaf or oafess in Rochester for a wretched display of timing.

I waited until the clocks in the information booth indi-

cated five of one, killing time and finally getting reassurance
my ears were still attached. Then I walked up the marble
staircase to the Vanderbilt Avenue exit, out through the taxi-
way, and onto the street, peering through the snow to find the
Yale Club. Spotted it right away, just off to my right, the
three-sided marquee with the blue bunting and the block Y
making it impossible to miss.

I went catty-corner across the street, dodging the trucks
and cabs, hustling for the shelter of the doorway. On the
southeast corner of the building there was a brass plaque that
caught my eye; risking more frostbite, I paused to read it. Put
there by the Daughters of the American Revolution, the
plaque informed readers that on this very spot during the
Revolutionary War, the patriot Nathan Hale had been cap-
tured by the British and taken away to be executed as a spy.
Helluva way for an amateur investigator to start a meeting.

I walked through the Yale Club foyer, brushing snow
from my topcoat and the briefcase I'd borrowed from Ellis,
not owning one of my own and not ever intending to. The
coatroom was in the rear, I remembered from the only other
time I'd been there—when a friend of The Pearl's invited us
there for cocktails so he could report in person on how that
"purty lil' thing was doin'" in the clutches of the Yankees.
Beau something or other. Highly forgettable.

I surrendered my topcoat to an elderly attendant, who
might very well have been around when Nathan got nabbed,
but held onto the briefcase with its small contents of envelope
and my notebook. I had to ask the location of the Men's Bar,
since The Pearl's inclusion on the previous visit had banished
us to another place upstairs, presumably out of the hearing of
the "grown-ups," who had important matters to discuss.

It turned out to be on the second floor, up a superb staircase, past some softly clacking stock-market ticker-tape ma-
chines, tucked into the far corner on the right. Despite the
hour of the day it was reasonably well populated, the two
bartenders working hard to meet demands. The walls were
covered with various sporting memorabilia, principally pic-

tures of assorted rowing teams and an occasional oar (or was it scull) hanging here and there.

At the rear of the bar, to the extreme left, a tall, heavy-set man was waving at me, beckoning me over. Do I look that much out of place, I wondered, walking over. After all, the gray flannel, the button-down collar, and the rep tie were reg-ular-issue Brooks; ought to fit right in.

"MacCallum, isn't it? Got you straightaway—it's the tan this time of year that does it. Too early for the Season. Sticks out like a beacon. A drink against the chill?"

"It's MacCardle, Mr. Melton, and, yes, a Bloody Mary, thank you."

"MacCardle, of course, thoughtless of me. Had a chap named MacCardle in our entry one year, from some dreary state in the Midwest. Relation of yours?"

"I don't think so, Mr. Melton. My people are basically from the Philadelphia area. Here let me get the drinks."

"Not in the Yale club, old boy. Program's simple here: write the order on the chit with your number, sign it, hand it in. No cash. Less mess that way. Oscar, take care of this, if you would. We'll carry them into the other room."

Drinks in hand, we walked next door into an enormous room, beautifully appointed in rich, dark woods, heavy car-peting, table-and-chair arrangements placed throughout. He chose one near a floor-to-ceiling window looking out onto Vanderbilt Avenue, the light from the small student lamp creating a small pool of warmth against the dark outside.

We settled in, drank the drinks, and reordered. Another Bloody Mary for me, a triple extra-dry vodka martini on the rocks with an olive for Bryant Melton. When they arrived he picked up the glass in both hands and said, "Now, MacCar-dle, what can I do for you? Mysterious mutual friend of mine and Laura's, you said. Well let's get on with it."

"Laura's dead. She was murdered a little over a month ago. I know I lied to you, but it seemed like the best thing to do at the time."

Melton was obviously shocked—from his expression—

but he reacted by piling into me. "Then you *are* with the police. I refuse to say another word until accompanied by my attorney. This interview is over. Despicable behavior, I must say."

"Probably. Manners were never my long suit. I'm not a cop, though—that part was true. Just an old friend of the family. Right now the police have a suspect they're perfectly satisfied with—her husband. All I'm doing is trying to tie up some loose ends, one of which is you. And speaking of manners, I've come a long way to talk to you. Seems to me it's only common decency on your part to hear me out."

"Very well, I'll listen, but that's all. Now be quick about it. Husband, eh, didn't know she'd married. Sordid sound to it."

I'd been prepared not to like Bryant Melton III, and he certainly wasn't making the job any harder. Somewhere in this world lived a wife and two children who presumably loved him—for reasons that certainly escaped me. The assuredness, the old school, patronizing attitude, the clipped "I'm in a hurry, stop wasting my time" speech—all confirmed the image I'd drawn of him from his letter. What I wanted to do was reach across the table and belt that smug facade. What I did was tell him the whole story, right up to the point of my discovery at the Racquet Club.

"Interesting, MacCardle, if you relish that sort of thing. I fail to see what it has to do with me, however. Please, get to the point—while you're at it, signal the waiter please, there's a good chap."

Good chap repressed a truly homicidal urge and signaled the waiter, switching to ginger ale for me on the theory it would be very poor form to be carried out of the Yale Club.

I'd also decided it was time to rock Melton off dead center, to crack that glib shell and see what lived behind it. I reached into the briefcase, extracted the Xerox copies of Laura's savings account passbook, and spread them out on the little table. I took Melton through the statements step by step, winding up with the Hampton theory of blackmail. Then

I extracted a copy of the letter he'd written to her and handed it across for him to acknowledge.

"So, Mr. Melton, if it was a case of Laura's blackmailing someone, that someone could very well be you. Sometimes people who are being bled get pretty desperate—even to the point of taking out the bleeder, either personally or by arrangement. I read in the paper the other day that two kids in Cleveland had their stepfather knocked off for sixty-five bucks. It's not very hard.

"You said you didn't want to talk without your attorney. That's your right. But there aren't any witnesses here, just the two of us. So level with me. Tell me why Bryant Melton the Third didn't just get promoted to Head Suspect. Do that for me, would you, Mr. Sincere?"

That ought to do it, I thought. Come on, Melton, it's open kimono time—no place to hide. I looked across the table, waiting for his reaction. And didn't get one, at least not right away. I began to wonder if he'd heard anything I'd said. He sat slumped in his chair, the copy of the letter framed in his big hands. Tears had formed in the corners of his eyes. As he began to speak in a low, trembling monotone, I realized he wasn't here, but rather somewhere back in time.

"I didn't mean it to happen, didn't plan on falling in love with her. I wasn't a chaser, hadn't ever been unfaithful, unlike so many of my friends. I met her at a client party. Thompson was their agency; I was doing a consulting project. When we were introduced I thought I'd been hit by lightning. Never happened to me before or since. We didn't talk to anybody else for the rest of the party. As soon as we could, we left the party and went to her apartment. I called my wife from there, told her I'd been called out of town, and that it might be a couple of days.

"I spent the next three days in bed with her; I got up only to eat or go to the bathroom. It was a magic time, as if we'd built our own private world. I told her things I'd never said to anyone before, did things I'd only read about. She made me feel so important—as a lover and as a man. It was as if we'd known each other all our lives—no secrets, no inhibitions, nothing held back—a time of sharing and giving and love, a magic time indeed. That was the beginning.

"The next year was more of the same. Weeknights in town, noon hours, occasional weekends—I used every means and excuse I could think of to be with her. I didn't know if my wife knew or even suspected—by then I didn't care. I was going to marry that girl, no matter the cost. I was going to capture the magic and make it go on forever."

Here he stopped, waving the attendant over for another round; I passed. His drink came and he drained half of it in a single swallow, the broken veins and capillaries showing red against the pallor of his face. Clearly this guy's no stranger to the sauce, I thought. Hope he can handle it—I really want to hear the rest.

"The magic didn't go on forever; maybe it wasn't supposed to, maybe I was naïve, maybe I didn't want to admit it was wearing out, but it was. I don't know when it started, but the constant togetherness began to come apart. From seeing each other every chance possible, we began to drift apart—finally to a point where I was lucky to see her once a week.

"The quality of the relationship was deteriorating, too. She was becoming more and more withdrawn—often morose, sometimes sullen. The naturalness, the gaiety, the making me feel like a king was gone. She began treating going to bed with me like a chore, something to be done quickly just to get it out of the way.

"When I asked her why, what was going wrong, she just withdrew further. I was afraid to push too hard, afraid if I did I'd lose her for good—which I didn't want to happen, no matter what.

"So, I put up with the moods, with her increased mentions of her 'other life' in Greenwich Village, with her increased use of drugs. When we first met, I don't think she'd even smoked grass. No more—now it was either that all the time or some little pills she had. I don't know what they were, but they could take her from blue to flying and back again to blue in hours, or until she took another one.

"She was involved with an Off-Off Broadway group in the Village, writing the score for a musical version of *Death of a Salesman*, for God's sake. Maybe that's where she got into the drugs and the other things she later told me about—I don't know. All I did know was that I was trying to hang on desperately, trying to take her away from that part of her life, trying to rebuild the magic any way I could."

Melton finished his drink, called for yet another, went on in a tone now slightly vodka-blurred.

"The end came when she told me she was pregnant, that I had to make good on all those promises, get the divorce, and marry her. I realized that what I would have done gladly a year ago, now didn't seem so attractive. The job of bringing her back, trying to rebuild what had been now seemed an impossible task.

"I said we were going too fast, that we ought to stop and think it over. I questioned whether she really wanted a baby, whether that was the right way for us to start. Suggested she think about an abortion, getting straight, starting fresh from there.

"Then she got really ugly—told me I wasn't so hot, in bed . . . or as a person. Said she wasn't even sure the baby was mine. She looked really dangerous to me, flying high on the pills, face twisted into a mask I'd never seen. She stumbled over to the desk, dug out a packet of pictures, threw them at me. Told me to take my choice . . . as a souvenir.

"They were awful pictures. Laura with men, Laura with women. Threesomes, foursomes, white people and black. Everything sick people could think of. I wanted to throw up. I got dressed and got out of the place quick's I could.

"I stayed away from her, no more apartment, no more telephone calls, no more Laura. Finally, I wrote the letter. End to it. Told her send me the bill. Never saw her again."

Now he looked at me head on, belligerently, the bloodshot eyes glaring. "Go ahead, MacCallum, MacCallister, whatever your name is. Subpoena me or anything you want. I loved Laura, then I hated her, but I didn't kill her. It would have been like killing part of me. Now go away and just leave me alone."

So I did; picked up the briefcase, walked out, paused at the door to look back at the man slumped in the chair, muttering. Sad, drunken, lonely man. On the downslide, by the look of it. Driven by his own devils, finding alternately hope and despair at the bottom of the bottle. Bound on a one-way trip to oblivion, doing his best to hasten the passage. God help you Bryant Melton III, I thought; better thee than me. Yes, we'll check into where you were when she was killed, someone will look over all your financial records. But I knew we'd find nothing—only more testimony to the end of a man.

On that depressing note, I left the Yale Club, went back to the hotel, ordered a room service dinner. I pecked at it, unable to eat, unable to wash away the afternoon, which clogged my throat, the recollections of a man going over the edge, apparently not caring. Eventually gave up, suddenly realizing how tired I was, how much the strain of the day had told on me.

Three weeks until the trial, Mr. Supersleuth, and now we're back to square one. Trying doesn't count—only results. We're mighty short in that department. Put it to bed, I thought, quit torturing yourself.

So I shucked off the clothes, climbed into bed, and went to sleep.

I woke up totally unrefreshed, the sour morning taste in my mouth matching the thoughts in my head. Might be nice to pull a Melton, I thought, just have eleven Bloody Marys for breakfast and call it a day—blot out the lousy memories. Escapist City.

Then I remembered Bucciarelli's party, the one I was supposed to be the guest of honor at, the one we'd set up by phone from Florida. Some guest of honor you'll be, laddie, about as welcome as the measles, in this state of mind. I couldn't skip it, though I wanted to, wanted to very much. Butch is a good friend, MacNumbnuts; he didn't bargain for any part of the new you. So get it together, go on over, shake the hands, smile periodically, try to act like a human being.

I phumfed around the room for the rest of the day, making a ritual out of sent-in breakfast, shaving, and showering. Later ordered up some beer and pretzels, sitting in my skivvies like a larger Archie Bunker, drinking the beer, eating the pretzels, watching ten very tall black men run, jump, and stuff the ball in the hoop, while the announcer made more noise than the crowd. The final score was a hundred and thirty something to a hundred and twenty something—as if anybody really cared.

Finally it was time to go to the party. I got dressed, left the Barclay, found a liquor store a block away. Bought a quart of George Dickel, that supersmooth bourbon The Pearl used to call "gen-u-wine, Tennessee sippin' whiskey." Got a cab, gave him Butch's address, settled back for the ride across town.

Butch has an apartment in a big sprawling building on upper Central Park West. Not the most fashionable address in the world but a great old building—high ceilings, marble and oak everywhere—like Butch, built to last.

The party was going full tilt when I got there, the cab driver grinning at the waves of noise hitting us as I leaned in to pay the fare. People were already overflowing the apartment, spilling out and sitting on the broad stairs that led to the ground floor. I edged my way in, trying not to trample or get spilled on, located Butch in the middle of the loudest group of revelers, roared at him almost happily. He beat on me enthusiastically, took the bottle from me, pointed to the bar, said I was on my own from there on, gave me an enormous ornate badge marked "Guest of Honor," insisted I pin it on.

I elbowed my way to the bar, got a drink, then navigated over to a wall where I could watch the carnage with at least my back protected. Several old friends came by, many drinks got poured, lots of new friends got made. I realized, with almost a guilty feeling, that I was having a fine time indeed. And, as a poet wrote, the best was yet to be.

Enter, stage right, one Mary Eleanor Phelan, a tiny, laughing elf of a girl with the bluest eyes in the history of man and an awe-inspiring brace of upper frontals that did wonders to the yellow cashmere turtleneck. Suddenly, I knew exactly where the Guest of Honor badge belonged; I only hoped I could pin it on without getting arrested.

Mary Eleanor Phelan, laugher at jokes, teller of tales, singer of Irish ballads, an absolute joy. We tiptoed past the desk of the Barclay, hand in hand, giggling like school kids, M.E. clutching the last bottle of Butch's champagne in her free hand.

Afterward, in the closeness of the bed, I wrapped myself around the small form, my right arm serving as her pillow. I dropped off that way, feeling warm and fond and slightly foolish.

Thanks, Butch. Thanks, M.E. You took the battered, faltering machine and made it run again. Blessings on you both, my unwitting Samaritans, you know not what you did.

17

I woke to her astride my midsection, her small fists beating softly but insistently on my chest. The black swing of hair moved about, barely concealing the eyes or other delightful parts of her, which I reached for with undisguised lust.

"Quit it, lout; save it for another day. It's almost nine. You've got just time enough to buy me breakfast and put me on the subway. I'm due at the station house at noon."

"Station house?"

"C'mon, stud, I'll explain it to you over breakfast."

Which she did, over an all-too short meal at the Brasserie—coffee and brioche for me, a longshoreman's breakfast for her. I didn't have to ask where she put it all, being fully aware of the incredible vitality and energy crammed into that compact frame.

Of all things, M.E. turned out to be a cop. A real, honest-to-goodness member of New York's Finest. One of the things we hadn't discussed last night was careers, it not being that sort of occasion. Anyway, I'm not sure I would have believed it even if she'd whipped out her badge.

I walked her to the subway, kissed her good-bye, promised to support the P.B.A. and to call her the next time I was in town. I watched her go down the stairs into the tunnel, stop to give me a final wave, and then disappear.

I looked at my watch, found out it was quarter of eleven, decided to walk up to Park Avenue and go to the eleven-o'clock service at Saint Bartholomew's.

Saint Bart's is a New York landmark, an imposing old church whose front runs the whole block between Fiftieth and Fifty-first Streets on Park Avenue, including a lovely little garden on the Fiftieth Street side. Incongruously, it sits surrounded by the citadels of capitalism: Citicorp, Barclay's Bank, the Waldorf, the Seagram's Building, and the Racquet Club. It predates all of them, the cornerstone dating to 1817, an ecclesiastic constant on one of the most expensive pieces of real estate in New York.

I went not only for the good it would undoubtedly work on my heathen soul, but also because I'd promised Billy I would look up his old seminary friend, Russell Hayes.

It all came back to me easily and forcefully, from the long-ago memories of Sunday-morning church with my brother, Mal, Mother, and Doctor Don. Little had changed, the order of worship much the same as in the days of Henry VIII, the words of comfort and challenge, underpinned with the stately hymns of the seventeenth and eighteenth centuries. This had been The Pearl's church, one she'd unsuccessfully tried to get me to attend. Now surrounded by rosewood and stained glass, the clear voices of the choir serenely carrying the melody, I wondered why I hadn't gone with her, and kicked myself for not even having tried.

After the service, I went around to the office on the Fiftieth Street side, made some inquiries, finally was directed to the Reverend Hayes. I introduced myself, and told him Billy sent his best.

His long face actually lit up, the eyes sparkling, the deep laugh lines stretching. "Billy, is it now? Well, of course, it had to be; sooner or later he had to get tagged with that one. Look, Mr. MacCardle, I've got some details to clear up here, but I'd love to hear more. Let's meet at Keenan's—Third and Forty-ninth—around two. They serve a terrific brunch. Can do?"

"Can do, Reverend. And the name's Cam."

"Russ, Cam. See you there."

So I went back to the hotel, bought the Sunday *Times*,

toted it upstairs, and had at it. I began with the Week in Review section, feeling sanctimonious about not having *started* with dessert, then I read the sports pages. Finally, I dove into the crossword puzzle, realizing after a struggle that I wasn't going to finish it in time. That's one deferrable monster, I thought; best to get over to Keenan's.

Not surprisingly, granted his relationship with Billy, Russ Hayes was like putting on an old shoe—pleasant, easy to talk to, knowledgeable on a wide variety of topics. I brought him up to date on Billy, took some mental notes on what Russ had been doing, for passing along. I touched lightly on why I was in the city, mentioning that Laura Morgan, then Laura Evans, had been a member of his church. He barely remembered her, noting that she left New York just about the same time he arrived, so they never really got to know each other.

The afternoon had skimmed by, the Guinness clock behind the bar indicating half-past six. On an impulse, I asked Russ if he was a hockey fan and told him I thought I could scare up a couple of seats for the Rangers–Bruins game. Russ said any kid from Belmont, Massachusetts, who wasn't a Bruins' fan was considered a social leper.

I made some phone calls, hit on the third try. We taxied over to the new (to me) Madison Square Garden, made a supper out of hot dogs and beer, and yelled like maniacs as the two teams battled below us, fittingly, to a 3–3 tie.

Then I dropped Russ off at Saint Bart's and went on to the Barclay. It took all of two minutes to get to sleep, savoring a most pleasant day.

Clean living pays off. Right, gang?

Right.

I called Phillip Corwin's office mid-morning. Miss Super-efficient said, yes, indeed, Mr. Corwin had returned. Yes, she'd given him the message. Yes, he'd be delighted to see me tomorrow at two, the eleventh floor, check in with the receptionist, please.

With the balance of the day to invest, I decided my

culture quotient was dangerously low. Went to the Guggenheim and the Frick. Had lunch at the Modern. Klee, Kandinsky, and Miró. Matisse, Modigliani, and Utrillo. All my favorites.

Went to a John Pike showing in a little gallery on Fifty-seventh Street. Pike does not yet have the stature of the art world superstars, but he was a master at watercolor—the most demanding form in which an artist can work. I'd met Pike at a party and had been completely charmed by him—a sturdy, square-shouldered artisan, whose large, rough hands seemed better suited to blacksmithing than turning out the fragile, delicate traceries that mark his work.

Capped off the day by having dinner with Hammerin' Henry and his wife, Estelle, at their apartment in Riverdale. Stell had been a magna at Cornell, continuing her education in the city while Henry made life unsafe for wide receivers—an interesting parlay if ever there was one. Ph.D. earned, she was now an assistant professor of politics at Barnard and very, very up on the comings and goings of the world. Talking to Stell was like playing tennis with John McEnroe—constant pressure from all sides, only the occasional desperate conversational lob giving me time to work on the superb duck à l'orange. She was also very funny, delivering some devastating commentary with an absolutely straight face. Commenting on an extremist politician, she said, "Every time that man opens his mouth, he subtracts from the sum total of human knowledge."

Go get 'em, Stell, all the fuzzy thinkers, everywhere. Stick it in their ear. Don't give up, ever. Somehow I knew she wouldn't.

Good night, Henry. Good night, Doctor Stell. Don't be strangers, hear?

I was swept into the Graybar Building on a tide of late luncheon returners, the executives all talking earnestly to one another, secretaries twittering about the spring showing at Bloomie's. I ran into a little culture shock at the elevator bank—a uniformed starter, spotless in gray, wearing a military hat with a shiny visor. I thought elevator men went out with the dodo. Not in the Graybar Building.

I got off at eleven in a crowd of most important people—must be where all the biggies live, I thought. I let them swarm by me and walked over to the receptionist, who was apparently handling an absolute *crisis* on the telephone, if what I could hear was any indication. Evidently order was finally restored because the telephone went down and the smile came on. I presented myself.

"Good afternoon. My name is MacCardle. I have a two-o'clock meeting with Mr. Corwin."

"Yes, sir. I'm afraid Mr. Corwin hasn't returned from luncheon yet. Just hang your coat in that closet over there and make yourself comfortable. I'll call Allison for you."

"Thank you, ma'am. I'll do that."

Allison, Allison. Had to be Miss Super-efficient. And so it was: tidy, tweedy, well-turned out—a page from the Lord & Taylor catalog. She took me in tow, marching me through a wide corridor of very impressive offices, each in a different style of furnishing, each doored with black, wrought-iron grill-work. We turned right at the end and walked all the way back to a corner office, where she ushered me in and asked if I would like a cup of coffee while I waited. I would, thank you very much, black, please. It came in a solid china mug, the like of which I had not seen since the Marine Corps. On its side the Cunard Lines seal in blue, the lettering indicating H.M.S. *Titanic*. Evidently, Corwin has a sense of humor, I thought. He'll need it. Allison left me to my coffee, assuring me Mr. Corwin knew all about the meeting and no doubt would be right along.

The delay gave me the chance to study his office. I am an incurable snoop. If you look at the titles in someone's bookcase you can get an idea of what kind of person you're dealing with. Offices must be even more revealing, I figured, particularly when done as nicely as these were. In keeping with the mug, his office looked like the captain's quarters on a ship, sea gray and white, offset with red leather chairs and couch, carpet in a deep navy blue. A huge mahogany desk was pushed against one wall, on it a picture of a stunning young woman. Laura? Time would tell.

I was admiring a particularly handsome print of the frigate H.M.S. *Ariadne*, bowling along under full sail out of Nevis, when he walked in the door.

The man was as squared away as the office—tall, spare, ruddy-faced, hazel eyes boring into me as he introduced himself. Carefully brushed silver hair, trim, aviator-frame glasses, gray pinstripe suit. A line from Gilbert and Sullivan popped into my head, "the very model of a modern major general," though in Corwin's case it would have been an admiral.

"Mr. MacCardle, sorry to be late. Client lunches have a habit of doing that, and after all, it is his money. Let me get Allison to bring us a jug of coffee and we'll get on with it. You said it had to do with Laura. Not trouble, I hope. Well, whatever it is, I'm sure we can set it right, eh?"

Not this time, sir, I thought, somewhat surprised by my reflexive use of the title. I didn't say anything, just handed him my copy of the letter he'd written over ten years before. He read it slowly, with no expression save the bunching of his jaw muscles, his mouth setting into a thin grim line. No tears from this one. Maybe in his own private sorrow place but not in public. The hazel eyes turned gunsights onto me. "Mr. MacCardle, there is only one way in the world for you to be in possession of this letter. Laura's dead, isn't she? I want to know *when, how, who*, and *what's* being done about it. Take all the time you want.

"Allison, cancel all my appointments for the balance of the day, shift anything big over to Mr. Robinson.

"Now, then. The whole story, please."

Instinctively liking the man and knowing I was talking about his only child, I gave him a cleaned-up version of the Laura Evans Morgan story. I gave him all the facts, how the police were holding Ralph, how Billy and Ellis and I were involved, what we and the police had done to date. It was a long story, but he listened patiently, sipping his coffee, occasionally taking notes on the legal pad on his blotter. When I got to the part about Hampton's theory on blackmail, he interrupted.

"The damn fool. That is, if she really was doing it. If she needed money, anytime, any amount, all she had to do was ask. She knew that. Waste, just waste. Dammit all, anyway."

I went on, finishing the story, amplifying the details, answering the questions he framed from his notes, wanting somehow to try to ease the pain I knew he felt. Outside it had grown dark; here the offices were closed and silent, the inhabitants gone for the day, as he thought through what I'd told him.

"This is a terrible day for me, Mr. MacCardle, worse than any I can remember. You're fortunate we don't live in ancient times; back then they *executed* the bearer of bad news."

I mumbled some kind of agreement, knowing he wasn't looking for a response, but admiring the strength of character that allowed even that small attempt at humor, at trying to keep things on an even keel.

"You know Laura's and my physical relationship; it's spelled out in the letter. What you don't know is how we got along. Which is to say, we didn't, although God knows I tried.

"She told me she was going to Florida, turned me down when I offered to put her up with friends of mine in Palm Beach. She wrote that she was getting married, and specifically asked me not to come because it would demand explanations she didn't want to give.

"I stopped writing to her because none of my letters were ever answered—I don't know if she even read them. She answered the telephone calls—I talked to her just two months ago, before I left the country—always polite, always noncommittal, never volunteering anything.

"It was as if she were ashamed of herself, of her parents

and of me—as if she didn't *want* to know the truth, couldn't or wouldn't accept it.

"It's been a heartbreaking task. No, don't feel sorry for me; it was what I had to do—or at least try to do. It seems the task is over.

"Apparently you and your friends and the police have done everything you could and I'm grateful, most grateful. I understand the decision not to hire a private investigator, although I'm willing to fund it if you change your mind.

"One thing I can do, and will do tomorrow morning first thing, is call your Lieutenant Hampton and post a fifty thousand dollar reward for any new evidence that helps find and convict her killer. Maybe it will stir something up, maybe not, but it's all I can think of from my end. Please make sure you leave me his telephone number.

"A final question, Mr. MacCardle, do you agree with the police that it was her husband's doing?"

"Sir, I just don't know what to believe anymore—if I ever did to begin with. My instincts tell me Ralph Morgan didn't do it, but that's all, just instincts. We can't prove his story any more than he can. And everything, everybody, that's turned up so far has been a dud.

"We won't stop trying, Mr. Corwin, please believe that. Also, please accept our sincere condolences. I didn't know your daughter, but Billy said she was a wonderful person and that's enough for me."

"Thank you, really, both for the promise and for the sentiment. It's funny, you know. I'd trade all this, trade anything I have for one more day of her life. Now, it's a trade I can't ever make.

"At the risk of being rude, I'll say good-bye now. I need to be alone for a while."

We shook hands. I walked out of his office and left Hampton's telephone number on his secretary's desk, where she'd see it straight off. Trudged up Lexington to the Barclay in light snow, aiming for the dark bar on the first floor for a drink and reflections on a good man that life had dealt a very poor hand.

The red light on the telephone was blinking as I walked into my room. Someone was trying to get hold of me; with any luck it was M.E. It wasn't. The message desk said a Mr. Bobby Evans had called at 3:10, wanted me to call back. Area code 904-555-5520. No, sorry, they didn't know where that was.

I dialed the unfamiliar number, heard it ring a dozen times with no answer, hung up the phone. Typical, I thought, just typical.

Then, on the theory that misery loves company, I called Dick Ellis at home to report my news or, more accurately, the lack thereof. Susan answered, telling me Dick was in Tallahassee on some kind of zoning hearing, would be back late tomorrow and was there anything she could do.

I said no, please tell him I was coming home, talk to him tomorrow, thank you very much, hope everybody's fine, see you soon.

I got Billy just as he was leaving for dinner, the round voice sounding as if he were next door. "Hello, Cam. How's life in the wicked city?"

"Not so great, pal, and not very productive either. Tell you more when I see you tomorrow—time to pack it in up here."

"That's too bad. Say, did Bobby Evans call you?"

"Yeah, I was just getting to that. He left a message, I called back, and he wasn't there. What's that all about? He doesn't even know me."

"I put him on to you. He's in Daytona, getting ready for the Five Hundred. He wanted me to go up there—said he'd gotten a telephone call from a lawyer in New York, had to do with some personal effects of Laura's."

"Personal effects? Sounds vaguely mysterious, Father Divine."

"He didn't know any more than that. Anyway, I can't get

up there. Father Michael has the flu and I have to mind the store."

"Want me to go?"

"Please. It may be nothing, but I told Bobby you could probably go see him. Call that number when you get to the airport. Somebody will come and get you—you're expected. And, good luck."

"It can't be worse than what we've had so far, Your Grace."

"Keep the faith, as we say in the priest business. See you."

Just what we needed, mysterious messages. Maybe we ought to try séances, I thought, stifling a guffaw at the thought of Lieutenant Hampton in a long robe with a pointed hat and crystal ball. Semi-hysterical.

Well, what the hell, you got something better to do, Bubba? Let's see what we can do about getting out of here.

It turned out to be much easier than I'd thought; evidently the traffic problem was more one-way than total. I got a seat on an Eastern section out of Montreal, leaving LaGuardia at 9:35 and arriving Daytona at half-past noon.

I sorted out the dirty laundry, packed the garment bag, and left a wake-up call for six.

Mysterious message, I mused. What do you suppose that could be? Like Scarlett O'Hara, we'd just have to face that tomorrow.

18

The big plane lifted off on time, roaring over Shea Stadium, out to the ocean, making a gentle, rolling turn to starboard, heading south.

Airplanes are wonderful places to think. There's nothing to do, no one to bother you, the biggest decision centering on whether to have another cup of coffee or not.

I used the time trying to answer the question, Who was Laura Morgan? It was the question I raised when I'd first gotten involved, when I'd said she had to be more than two-dimensional. Trouble was, now she had so many dimensions she was hard to shape—like those early 3-D movies where the cardboard glasses they gave you fell off.

The warp of the fabric of her life was straightforward; it was the woof, the filled-in part, that was driving me nuts. Upper-middle-class girl graduates from college, works in New York, has a broken love affair. Goes to Florida to recuperate, meets a man there and marries him. Joins a church, joins a tennis club, has a best friend, gives piano lessons. Has some problems with her marriage, but who doesn't? So things are rocking right along, then up comes unlucky December the thirteenth and she gets snuffed.

Why?

Who *was* Laura Morgan?

I tried a variation on Hampton's yellow-pad discipline. Made a column of people whose lives she'd influenced positively, another for those she hadn't. Scrapped that exercise because so many names showed up in both columns.

Then I tried it another way, listing all her good points on one side, less than good on the other, studied it and decided I'd just drawn a character analysis of almost everybody. She wasn't two-dimensional, but none of us are.

To Bryant Melton she was Evil. To Billy and to Betty Hillson she was a Saint. Everyone else fell somewhere in the middle of those two extremes.

I wondered what would happen if I dissected myself the same way, and concluded it would probably come out pretty much like Laura: a mixture of good traits and bad; a combination of accomplishments and lost opportunities; friends, enemies, and lots of people who didn't give a Chinese damn one way or the other.

Who was Laura Morgan? Apparently, she was Everyman. But who would kill Everyman, and why?

Perhaps the police were right. Maybe Ralph *had* killed her. Certainly we hadn't turned up a better candidate, and it didn't look very hopeful we would. Maybe there wasn't a better candidate. Wouldn't that be ironic? All this chasing around when the real killer was already in jail. Then how did you explain the blackmail pattern? Maybe it, like the phantom strangler, was also an illusion. Or maybe it was real, but not directly related.

Would we ever know the truth? Would we have the chance to find it before time ran out for Ralph Morgan? The sour thought kept returning—maybe time *should* run out on him, I don't know, maybe they had the right man all along.

The Fasten Seat Belt sign came on, followed almost immediately by the No Smoking sign, as the stew announced our approach to the Daytona airport. Speculation would have to wait—at least for now.

The big, digital clock/thermometer said it was seventy-one degrees, not sweltering but a welcome change from the damp cold of New York. I collected my garment bag, walked

down the steps, across the tarmac, into the terminal. I went to
the bank of telephones, dug in my pockets for change, and
called the number Billy had given me.

"Afternoon, SNAVE Racing."

"Good afternoon, I'm trying to reach Bobby Evans."

"He's over to the garage area right now. Take a message?"

"I was told to call this number, my name's MacCardle—"

"Why didn't you say so first thing? We're waitin' on you.
You at the airport now?"

"Uh-huh."

"Well, just stay right where you are. We'll be by the
front door to get you, 'bout twenty minutes. We got a red,
white, and black van with a big gold thirty-five wrote on the
side—cain't miss us. Stay there, hear?"

"Thanks."

A "red, white, and black van with a big gold thirty-five
wrote on the side" shouldn't be too hard to spot, even for
you, I thought. It wasn't either, arriving almost twenty minutes to the dot after I'd called, swinging up to the front door,
letting off an absolute giant of a man. I judged him at about
six-ten, two-eighty at least, with shoulders, as The Pearl used
to say, "about two ax handles wide."

"Hi-dee, Mr. MacCardle, welcome to Day-tona. M'names
Boomer Mays. Sure is a pleasure to meet you. Saw you play a
hunnerd times on the TV, I bet."

"Hi, Boomer, thanks. The name's Cam."

"Okay, Cam, just give me that there bag and hop in the
back. You be more comfortable there."

As if I dared refuse.

On the way to the track, Boomer asked me if I'd ever
been to Daytona before. I told him I hadn't, but I was certainly looking forward to it. He said they were coming up on
Speed Week, the one time a year when the town really got
turned upside down. It featured every kind of racing imaginable, culminating in the Daytona 500, the Super Bowl of
stock-car racing. I noticed all kinds of banners—the general

ones heralding WELCOME TO DAYTONA—HOME OF NASCAR, CELEBRATE SPEED WEEK; WELCOME RACING FANS. There were sponsors' banners everywhere as well, creating a riot of colors in the streets. Union Oil, Champion, Gatorade and Mountain Dew, STP and Wrangler, and on and on. A true carnival atmosphere.

Inside, the track was a whole new world, rendered on a scale to take your breath away. I found out later the Speedway was built on 455 acres, with a 44-acre lake smack in the middle of it. Along the north side, just behind us, there were nine permanent grandstands. Boomer said they could put seventy thousand people there, and it certainly looked it. He also said, come Speed Week, there'd be another seventy-five to a hundred thousand people camped in the infield, right where we were currently driving.

The van kept on, raising a rooster tail of dust behind us, then pulled right, through a set of gates marked "Garage Area." Suddenly, we were surrounded by people, drivers in their flame-retardant suits and helmets, pit crews in colorful uniforms, NASCAR officials, and just plain people. Lots and lots of people.

We pushed ahead slowly through the crowds, a friendly thumping on the van's sides as people recognized it, down the length of a row of garages and into a tiny compound enclosed with hurricane fencing. Inside the compound was a low, small cement-block building, a red, white, and black SNAVE flag gently flapping on the flagstaff.

"This here's home for us, Cam. Damn sight better than squattin' around the garage. Cain't hear nothin' over there neither. We was lucky to get this place. A company dropped out of racin' couple of years ago, and Bobby just grabbed it up. Ain't real fancy, but it does for us."

Inside was just as Boomer had described it, plain but very functional. There was a big room with couches and chairs that had seen far better days, a battered refrigerator in one corner. Off the main room was a small office with two wooden desks crammed into it. Boomer went to the refrigerator, took out two cans of beer, gestured to the bigger of the two couches.

"Might's well wait on him here, Cam. Bobby be practicin' now, prob'ly quit around four. It's the first year for us in them down-size jobs. Bobby says we're gettin' squirrely up in turn two, need to work on the suspension some. They'll go awright; deal is to keep 'em glued down. Know much 'bout racing'?"

I told him I knew next to nothing about racing, but I'd like to know more as long as he kept it simple so my small brain could understand.

He grinned and gave me an hour's worth of the short course for beginners. The Winston Cup Circuit, the major leagues of stock-car racing. Thirty events, coast to coast, mostly on Sunday afternoons. Run on a whole variety of tracks, from the small ones at Martinsville and Nashville to the twister at Riverside, California, up to the monsters at Charlotte, Talladega, and Daytona, where speeds often reached two hundred miles an hour. As he talked, out spilled the names of the NASCAR greats—King Richard Petty and his heir apparent, son Kyle, Cale Yarborough, David Pearson, Buddy Baker, Bobby Allison, and a rising group of new superstars, Darrell Waltrip, Dale Earnhart, Terry Labonte, Ricky Rudd —names I'd heard dimly on "Wide World of Sports" but now, according to Boomer, I was about to meet.

"All them people be through here by the day's end. Bobby got a lotta friends and the place is so handy and all."

Shortly before five o'clock, the crowd gave way slightly and Boomer jumped up.

"*There* he is. Hi-dee, boss, this here's Cam MacCardle."

"Cam, nice to meet you. Thanks for coming up. We'll go back in the office and talk in just a minute. I got a couple of things to do first.

"Boomer, I damn near lost us a car just now. I was running with Petty through the four turn pretty as you please, pulled out to pass him, and thought I was going over the wall. It's either that damned new spoiler or we ain't got the suspension dialed in right. We got a lot of work, boy, first thing tomorrow, you hear me? Do me a favor now and get me a Pepsi out of that box. I'm dry as a damn bone. Get Cam another Busch too, huh, bring 'em back to the office? Thanks, buddy."

Bobby pushed his way through the crowd, pulling me along, into the little office in the back, taking the cans from Boomer and closing the door, producing an almost-unnatural quiet compared to the din outside.

"Busch and Pepsi are NASCAR sponsors, so we try to pay them back a little. Hope the beer's okay for you."

"Just fine, thanks. By the way, I appreciate the airport pickup and the mother hen job Boomer did."

"He's something else, isn't he? Talk your damn ear off, give him half a chance. Folks call us Mutt and Jeff, him bein' so big and all and me bein' no-account size."

Bobby *was* small, much smaller than I'd expected, probably around five-six or seven. But he was built solidly, wide shoulders, thick neck, big chest, abnormally large hands. I guessed he needed all of that wrestling those monsters around the tracks at those kinds of speeds.

"Bobby, somethings been puzzling me all afternoon—what's SNAVE stand for?"

"That's an easy one. Racin's a funny business. Chicken one day, feathers the next. When I finally got to the chicken part, my accountant up in Greenville got me to incorporate. Had all kinds of fancy titles picked out. I figured keep it simple—SNAVE is just my name spelled backward, see?"

"Of course. Pretty dumb of me not to spot it."

"No. Lot of people ask that, don't feel bad. Listen, Cam, let me tell you why I called Reverend Graham and then we'll clear up some housekeeping details. I got a call from a lawyer in New York Monday morning. Fella named Greenspan, Greenberg . . . I forget. He's with the law firm that handled my folks' estate. Don't know how the hell he found me, went through the NASCAR people, I guess. Anyway, he was at a

party Saturday night and ran into a friend of his named
Melton—"

"I know *him*. I talked to him in New York last week. He
and Laura were . . . friends."

"Yeah, well, I guess they were all three friends. This
Melton guy asked the lawyer if he had heard Laura was dead.
Took the lawyer back some, I guess. He hadn't heard word
one. But he did remember Laura sent him a package about a
year ago. Asked him to put it in his safe-deposit box. The
lawyer said it's just a little package, addressed to me, with a
note on it asking him to send it to me in Greenville if anything
ever happened to her. He told me he sent it Express Mail so
he'd have a record of it and was that all right? I told him
sure—I'd get Raymond to sign for it at the condo office. He'll
dump it in my mail slot. I promised to call him when I got
home and tell him what it was. And that was the conversation. It may be nothing, Cam. I mean, Laura was such a sentimental person, it's likely something of Mother's or Dad's she
wanted me to have. But you never know, and if it might help
you fellas you ought to have a look.

"I got my hands full tomorrow. If we get the car going
right Friday afternoon we could take the plane over to Greenville, pick up the package, be back here by suppertime. All
right with you?"

"Better than all right. Boomer's got me fascinated with
this whole racing thing. Promised to run me around the track
tomorrow, if there's time. The package will keep till then."

"Good, then that's all set. Now, about the housekeeping
chores. We got you a room at the Holiday Inn on the beach,
where we are. Leave your stuff in the van; Boomer'll take it
over and check you in. You're having dinner tonight with Ben
Reed and his wife, Sally. Ben used to run the show at Dover,
Delaware; now he's got a big job at NASCAR. Knows everybody. They're two of the all-time nice people of the world—
you'll love them both. They'll pick you up here around six-
thirty, take you to dinner, run you back to the hotel.

"I'll meet you for breakfast in the coffee shop around seven—long day for us field hands. I'd like to join you for dinner, but I can't. Been ducking a reporter from *Motor Sports Illustrated* and she finally ran me out of excuses. I've got to give her some kind of interview or she'll make me look like the all-time bad guy in that rag. Guess you know all about that, eh?"

"More than I care to remember. That all sounds great, Bobby. Again, thanks for all the trouble."

"My pleasure. Now, I'm goin' to get cleaned up. Boomer will get you anything you want while you wait."

The Reeds came by right on time, scooped me up, took me to a medium-size dinner put on by the Pontiac people. Within three minutes, it was Ben, Sally, and Cam—every bit as nice and fun as Bobby had said. I was sorry when the evening was over, like coming to the last page of a book you really enjoyed. Ben said he'd come by the SNAVE place the next day. Sally said she had *lots* better things to do than that, but maybe we could get together later.

They dropped me at the hotel, I picked up my key at the desk and walked up the stairs whistling. Like a kid with a new toy, I could hardly wait until tomorrow.

19

"Good morning, Mr. MacCardle, it's six-oh-three, the weather forecast for greater Daytona is clear and warm, have a good day."

My wake-up call.

When I'm awake at six—which is very seldom—it usually means time to turn over and go back to sleep. But not today. Today was a working day for Bobby and his crew—a play day for me.

It was a day to be spent wandering around the track, watching the brightly colored racers challenge the high-banked turns, as the practice-lap speeds kept building toward two hundred. A day to be spent poking into the garages, talking with the pros who built these cars and made them go. A day to pick up more of the history and folklore of the sport from Boomer—maybe a day to take a ride around the course at speed. Then, hopefully, drinks and dinner with Ben and Sally Reed to finish it off. Tomorrow would be time enough to get back into the investigation business. Today was for R and R—racing and recreation.

I walked over to the window, pulled the curtain back, peered outside. The operator had been right on—not a cloud in the dawn sky. Probably be in the eighties today, better dress light.

This one's a top-drawer Holiday Inn, I thought—adjustable shower head and big, fluffy bath sheets, not the usual, skimpy, thin towels you can't wrap around you. The cold, fine-spray setting got rid of the last of the cobwebs. Bath sheet knotted at the hip, I padded to the television set for some company while I shaved. Too early for the network, but somebody would be there to talk to me. There were two somebodies—a pinched, earnest young woman in a flowery print dress and a dough-faced man in a hymn to polyester. They were telling me all about the latest crisis in one of the banana republics, mangling the Spanish names and terms in the flat, nasal drawl of North Florida. I turned up the volume so that it would carry into the bathroom.

I patted on the shaving lather, rinsed my hands, was reaching for the razor when I started tracking what Ms. Earnest was saying: "—partment spokesperson confirmed there are no leads as to the whereabouts of the person or persons unknown responsible for the murder. Reporting again, racing driver Bobby Evans has been found shot to death at the Sea Breeze Inn in Ormond Beach. Stay tuned to Channel Ten for 'Eyewitness News at Seven.'"

I ran to the television set, started twisting the dial to other channels, hoping to pick up more. No help from the other two available stations—one was featuring an ancient Tom and Jerry cartoon, the other wrapping up their farm report. I flipped back to Channel 10, sat on the bed, and waited an interminable twenty minutes for the seven o'clock news, hoping against hope that maybe I'd heard wrong.

Bobby's murder was the third item and there weren't many details. Ormond Beach. Sea Breeze Inn. Body discovered by the night manager. Police withholding all other information pending a full investigation. "No, Isabel, that's all they'll tell us for now, back to you at the desk."

Mindlessly, I snapped the television off, wandered around the room trying to make some kind of sense of what I'd just heard. I didn't do very well. Shock and disbelief kept getting in the way of all my attempts to sort things out, logic no match for all the unanswered questions. A thought kept trying to beat its way through all the Jell-O in my head.

It was something Bobby had said before he left last night.

Something about an interview with a reporter from some magazine. But what the hell was it? Motor something. *Motor Sports Illustrated*. That's more like it. Maybe that's why he was in Ormond Beach; maybe that's got something to do with his getting killed. Better tell the cops. Now. Sure seems like more than what they have.

Whoa, laddie, hold the phone. There are better ways to let them know. You go busting in there with your little tidbit and they say, "Thank you, public-spirited one, please plan on sticking around for a month or so while we clean this up."

Meanwhile there was a very good chance somebody in authority would think to seal off the SNAVE office, his condominium, and everything else with the name Evans on it. That means, so long mysterious package, whatever you are, and isn't that why Bobby wanted to see you to begin with?

No, the smart money said to get to Greenville, pronto, so I set about doing just that. I quickly finished shaving, picked up the Yellow Pages, and found the number for Eastern Airlines.

"Greenville/Spartanburg? Yes, sir, we have a flight leaving Daytona at ten-thirty, arriving Atlanta eleven-twenty-one. Change to a twelve-forty-eight flight on Pinehurst Airlines, arriving Greenville/Spartanburg one-thirty-eight. Will that be first class or coach?"

Luck, pure dumb luck—the finest kind.

I got dressed, packed up, tore a sheet off the message pad, and scrawled a note to Boomer.

Dear Boomer,
    Can't tell you how sorry I am; he was a very nice guy. Let me know if I can do anything to help.
    I've gone home. If you need me you can get me at 305-555-3992.
    Please tell the police Bobby gave an interview last night to a reporter from *Motor Sports Illustrated* magazine. May be nothing, but didn't sound like they have a whole helluva lot to go on.

Sorry, again.
Cam MacCardle

I walked downstairs, checked out, and asked the clerk to put the note in Mr. May's box. It didn't seem very bright to hang around the lobby, so I took a cab to the airport, paid for my ticket, and spent the next hour plus trying to read a newspaper over my breakfast of coffee and sausage biscuits.

I couldn't concentrate on the paper or the breakfast. A day that had promised so much had turned to horror. The questions came hammering back at me. I couldn't believe Bobby Evans had an enemy in the world, but he obviously did. Who? And why? Was there any connection to Laura's death? It was beginning to look like open season on the Evans family. If there *was* a connection, what could it possibly be? They'd scarcely seen each other over the last fifteen years, not since he'd joined the Army. What could tie them together now? I realized the public-address system was calling my flight.

The trip to Atlanta and on to Greenville was a continuation of my breakfast confusion. Thoughts, counterthoughts, theories, and questions—all in a totally indigestible mental stew. I hoped there was, somewhere in this world, a wiser head than mine who could make some semblance of sense of it all. Somehow.

The Greenville/Spartanburg airport was a real surprise. I hadn't known what to expect, having never even heard of Greenville, or Spartanburg for that matter, before Bobby. It was a modern building, all white and glass, beautifully landscaped, with working fountains here and there.

I walked across the main lobby, went down a long escalator to the ground floor, looked around for the rental car counters. Found them off to the right—Hertz, National, and Avis. Just before going over there, I stopped at a line of telephone booths by the escalator, looked up Bobby's address in the telephone book. Evans, Robert L., 940 E. Pelham Road.

The only Robert Evans in the book—had to be him. Hope-fully.

I picked National, not because I didn't want them to "Try Harder" or let me "Fly Through Airports," but for a far more solid reason. Billy saves Green Stamps; only National gives them. So there, all you marketing biggies.

"Good afternoon, miss. I need four things from you. A car, of course, mid-size, if you have one. A recommendation on where to spend the night. How to get there. And how to get to 940 East Pelham Road. Can you do all that for me?"

"The first three, yes. The fourth I'll need help on. Prom-ise not to tell anyone; I'm a transplanted Yankee—only been here a month. Let me get Larissa. Meanwhile, we'll need your driver's license and a major credit card, please."

"Your secret's safe with me, Carpetbagger."

Between the Carpetbagger and Larissa, they did a good job of sorting me out—an Olds Cutlass and a map indicating how to get from the airport to a Ramada Inn on Pleasantburg Drive.

"Pelham Road's easy from the Ramada, Mr. MacCardle. Go north about four miles and you'll run right into it, on the right, real simple."

I drove through the college-campuslike outskirts of the airport, turned right on I-85, followed their map, hit the Ramada first time. Checked in, asked them to take my bags up to the room, got back in the car, and went looking for 940 East Pelham Road.

It was just four o'clock by the dashboard digital as I pulled onto Pelham Road, the shadows beginning to lengthen, cool enough to warrant putting the car heater on low. Not much time to find this place in daylight, I thought.

A large, weather-beaten gray sign marked the entrance to the complex. Boxwood Landing—940 East Pelham Road. So far so good. Unlike Florida, the entrance wasn't blocked off by a guard's booth. More good news—no need for identi-fication or explanations.

Boxwood Landing was a series of connected town houses, all in different colonial styles and trims, looking like a transplanted section of Georgetown or Beacon Hill. They wound up a road, through woods, and out of sight. Not so good. I had no way of knowing which was Bobby's. Go poke your nose in, chum, something will come of it; you can always rap on a door or two.

I was spared that chore. Halfway up the hill I saw a boy walking along, huge sack of newspapers slung over his shoulder, faded lettering on the side of the sack, *Greenville News-Piedmont.* Bingo.

"Excuse me, wonder if you could help me out?"

"I can try, sir."

"Which one of these houses is Mr. Evans?"

"You mean Bobby Evans, the race driver? It's number eighty-nine, all the way to the end, the green one. You a friend of Bobby's, sir? He's the greatest."

"Yes, son, I'm a friend. Thanks."

"Yes, sir."

Evidently the news hadn't reached Greenville yet, or I'd hit a kid who didn't watch the tube or read his own paper. Either way, he'd be one sad boy when he found out.

I parked in front of Bobby's unit, walking up the flagstones to the front entry, in the last light of day. Now comes the tricky part—hope Hampton has enough clout to spring me if I get busted for breaking and entering. Let's hope the absence of a guard shack is a good omen—I'd come a long way to lose to a dead-bolt lock.

I took my American Express Gold Card and slid it between the jamb and the edge of the door, at handle height, pushing with the left hand at the same time. The door popped open, slamming against its backstop, rebounding so that I had to catch it from closing again. Bang on, Mr. Malden. *Don't* leave home without it.

There was a jumble of mail on the floor, partly scattered when I pushed open the door. I snapped on the hall light switch and saw the Express Mail envelope right away, the orange and blue markings helping it stand out among the mass of letters, magazines, and circulars that had accumulated. The upper-left corner of the label bore the legend Smith, Fine, & Morse, Attorneys at Law, 15 Broad Street, New York, New York.

I picked it up, flipped off the light, closed the door firmly. Got in the car, turned on the headlights, observed the speed limit very carefully all the way back to the Ramada Inn. Helluva note if this turns out to be an old watch, Mr. Private Eye.

It wasn't an old watch.

I tore open the sealed gray envelope inside the express packet and shook its contents out on the bed. There were three filmstrips, thirty-five millimeter, black and white. And another, smaller envelope, also addressed to Bobby.

I looked at the filmstrips first, holding them up against the lamp on the desk. Pornography is fine if that's what gets to you, I thought. There were some truly inventive games going on in this lot. It would take amplification to identify the players, but no imagination was needed to figure out what they were doing.

Suddenly, I remembered my conversation with Bryant Melton and his mention of Laura's souvenirs. No. She wouldn't have sent those to Bobby. Why would she do that? A shattering of illusions? A final write-off, a "to hell with you, cruel world" gesture?

I opened the letter, read it slowly—then read it again. A sad letter, written in pain, reflective of the misery the human soul is capable of inflicting on itself.

Now I knew who Laura Morgan was, now the pieces began falling together swiftly, the pattern taking recognizable shape. It all made sense, a crazy, mournful, twisted sense.

Poor, sad soul. One last attempt to be heard, to be noticed—to establish some form of control, some inner direction before all the dreams were swept away. Not an angel, not a devil—just a human gone awry.

*　　*　　*

I telephoned Ellis—Susan answered. "Hi, Cam, Dick just got home. He'll be with you in a second."

"Where the hell are you, boy? The news about Bobby's all over the papers and the television. You in Daytona?"

"As a matter of fact, Counselor, I'm in Greenville, South Carolina."

"Greenville? Why?"

"Long story, Dick. Not a pretty one."

"You sound really down. You all right?"

"I am down. Shouldn't be, but I am. I think we've got the answer on who killed Laura Morgan and why."

"Unbelievable! Who?"

"Not now, it's too long a story and I need something that projects thirty-five-millimeter filmstrips."

"When can you get here?"

"I checked with the airlines. The best they can do is get me to Lauderdale by around five-thirty tomorrow. We'll just have to go from there."

"How sure are you? Enough to go to Hampton?"

"Very, very sure."

"Then the hell with it, charter a plane. It's only about a three-hour flight to the Boca airport—get you here by noon without trying hard. Call me only if you can't do it. Otherwise, I'll pick you up around twelve with a projector and we'll go see Hampton."

"Whatever you say, Counselor."

"Cheer up. Sounds like you did an outstanding job."

"Yeah. See you, Dick."

20

The sleek little Falcon jet roared down the runway at Greenville/Spartanburg airport, lifting off like a fighter plane, howling over the foothills of the Blue Ridge, turning south for home. I'd never flown in a plane this size, the sensation of the flight quite different from commercial aircraft. Not frightening, more a feeling of exhilaration—smooth, very, very smooth.

When we leveled off, high over Georgia, one of the pilots slid back the folding door to the flight deck and asked if I wanted coffee. He opened a small cabinet door set into the bulkhead, pushed a button, drew cups for both of us, came back, and sat opposite me.

"First flight in one of these, Mr. MacCardle?"

"Yeah. I love it. Haven't had so much fun since the hogs ate Grandma!"

"They're fun to fly, too. Very light on the controls, quicker than sin. The first series were all made in France, called the Mystere. Changed the name to Falcon for the U.S. Guess they figured no corporate exec wanted to fly around in something named Mystery. "

"I can see their point. Anyway, it's just terrific."

"Can't see much from up here. There's a jump seat in the cockpit. If you like, I'll call you on our approach to Boca; you can come up and shoot the landing with us."

"Great, long as I won't be in the way."

"No problem. Gotta go forward. Tell you when it's about time to land."

I sat back in the seat, put my stockinged feet up where the pilot had been, drinking coffee, feeling terribly self-important. Me, the president of U.S. Steel, and Arnold Palmer—yes, sir, the *only* way to fly.

Last night's black mood had passed, replaced by a determination to finish the thing strong, armed with the first real help so far. How fortunate we'd been, I thought, our progress much more a function of good luck than good management.

If Melton hadn't run into the lawyer, if the lawyer hadn't remembered the package, if he hadn't wanted a receipt for it's transmittal, if the police had sealed off Bobby's condominium, if there'd been a dead-bolt lock. If, if, if. I suddenly remembered an old Don Meredith "Monday Night Football" line. He'd said to Cosell, "Howard, if 'ifs' and 'buts' were candy and nuts, we'd all have a helluva Christmas."

I began mentally putting together a presentation for Lieutenant Hampton. I debated whether to use his "What We Know" format and talked myself out of it. He might think we were being smart ass. We'd played straight with him from the beginning and he'd been very helpful, so probably best for us to end up the way we began, particularly since the blackmail concept had been his all along.

I had it pretty well framed in my mind when the folding door opened again, the pilot beckoning to me to come forward.

"We're over Palm Beach now. Winds are northerly. We'll fly a long approach leg down the coast, turn right for a base leg, right again for the final. Just pull that handle there, yeah, the red one. That's it. Lock those two braces. Good. Now swing the cabin door shut. All set? Here we go."

The cockpit was crowded, but the view superb as we skimmed down the coast. I began picking out landmarks, seen only before at sea from the deck of the *Folly*. Lake Worth, Lantana, Boynton Beach, Delray. We swung west just past the tower of the Boca Raton Club, losing altitude, lining up for landing. The airport came up off to our right, postage-stamp size at first, getting bigger in a hurry. Now the runway, dead ahead, black-streaked from the tires of hundreds of landings. The pilot pulled back slightly on the wheel, the Falcon's nose came up, flared, and we kissed the ground with almost no impact, juddering down the runway as the pilot braked and cut in the reverse thrusters on the jets.

We were home. Time to go to work.

Sergeant Serkin met us in the lobby at two, led us upstairs to a small conference room that was dominated at one end by a movie screen. Said once we were set to go, he would fetch Lieutenant Hampton. Not knowing how many people might be involved, I asked him for half a dozen Xerox copies of Laura's letter, which he brought back just as I finished setting up the projector.

"All squared away?"

"Yes, Sergeant, you can call Lieutenant Hampton any time now."

I sat beside the projector, filmstrips and the stack of letters in front of me. The door opened and Hampton strode in—all business as usual—trailed closely by a short, stocky man in a blue pin-striped suit. Dick was out of his chair, walking over to shake hands.

"Hey, Elton, how you doing? Long time no see."

"*Has* been a long time, Counselor. Baldwin trail, I think. How's Susan? Kids?"

"Fine, fine Elton, meet my friend, Cam MacCardle. Cam's been the bird dog for us this time. Cam, meet Elton Bassett, assistant district attorney."

"Mr. Bassett."

"Mr. MacCardle."

It being his turf, Hampton chaired the meeting, setting its tone with his opening remarks. "Now that we have all the social la-di-da out of the way, let's see what you brought us that's so all-fired important, MacCardle. I want to warn you, though—I'm a busy man and Mr. Bassett's even busier. If this turns out to be foolishness, you're gonna think a safe fell on you."

I went through the little presentation I'd rehearsed on the plane, updating him on my New York trip, my meeting with Bobby Evans, and all the subsequent events. When I got to the illegal-entry part, he stopped me. "For the sake of my colleagues up in Greenville, we'll pretend we didn't hear that. Okay with you, Mr. Bassett?"

"Hear what?"

"Go on, MacCardle."

I told them what I'd found, mentioned that I had copies of the letter for all of us to review, suggested the letter would make more sense if we looked at the film first.

Dick turned the lights down and I began feeding the first filmstrip into the projector, frame by frame, twelve to a strip, thirty-six in all. Pornography is a big industry, so there must be lots of people who get satisfaction from it, but only the real hard-core sickos would appreciate these, I thought, my revulsion mounting with each new frame.

The photographer had been most professional, though; there was clearly only one star of the show—featured prominently in each picture—with a crowd of supporting players and exotic paraphernalia.

The last was the worst. She was on all fours, facing the camera, hair tucked into a black leather helmet, a studded collar around her neck. Her breasts pointed at the camera, large and full, the nipples grown extended, rigid. Her head was thrown back, in an expression of ecstasy or agony—collar in the huge hand of the black man ministering to her from behind. Her eyes were closed in this one, but there was no mistaking the high cheekbones, the jawline, the aristocratic nose.

Elaine Edwards, now Elaine Paley, known to friends as Pookie. Wife, wealthy socialite, rising political candidate. Star of the sick, pathetic little show.

Dick turned the lights back up and we sat staring at one another. Having read the letter, I'd had some idea what to expect, but the reality of it had shocked me almost as much as the others, who'd had it thrown at them cold.

Bassett broke the silence. "Jesus H. Mahogany Christ. I've known Forrest Paley for over twenty years. A look at just one of those would kill him sure."

"Not exactly what the Moral Majority would pick for a campaign poster," Dick said.

Hampton added, "Those pictures in the wrong hands could cause a *heap* of trouble around here. Be the end of her for fair—marriage, career, friends, the whole shooting match."

It was my cue to go on and I did. "They *were* in the wrong hands, Lieutenant. Your blackmail theory was right. Laura Morgan began threatening Mrs. Paley with these more than a year ago. It's spelled out in her letter."

I passed each of them a copy of the letter and the room became quiet as they read it—I knew its contents by heart.

My Dearest Brother.
    If you read this letter you will know that I am dead. Please try to find it in your heart to mourn me. I need someone to care. The films are of a two-timing slut named Elaine Paley. You can burn them or do anything you want; it won't make any difference anymore.
    All my life I've felt I was the one who got left out, the one everybody ignored, never good enough, always second best.
    It was pure hell living with Mum and Dad after you went away. You were their favorite child and they never let me forget it.
    Then they died and made us both orphans, until I found out Uncle Phil, my godfather, was my real father—only he didn't have the guts to say so when it counted. It made me feel doubly betrayed, by Mother and by him—not good enough again.
    I leaned on Elaine—how it hurts to write that name. Only she had taught me what real love could be. I went out with boys—drunken, pawing animals—but all the time it was

Elaine I wanted and turned to in the night. For the first time I felt really wanted, really worthwhile, a major part of someone's life.

She left me too; she wouldn't work in New York where we could be together, she had to go back home. New York was horrible, like college all over again. The vacation she spent with me was heaven, just like old times—until she left.

I thought I could learn to live without her. I fell in love with a man, really in love, just like normal. When he found out I was pregnant he dumped me. No husband, no baby, nothing—emptiness once more. The friends I had in the Village helped some, but it was always her.

I tried, but I couldn't stand it. I called her and said I was coming to Florida, that we could make it all right again, and we did—better than ever before.

I couldn't accept it when she announced she was getting married. I cried, tried every way to talk her out of it, but no use. Big, hairy, disgusting beast, Forrest Paley. The thought of him pressing his body against my dear sweet love made me want to throw up. I cried through the whole wedding.

I married Ralph to spite her, to show her she wasn't the only one who could be unfaithful. He's such a simp. And terrible in bed. No loving, no tenderness, just wim, wam, woom, like I ought to be grateful. I'll fix his little wagon too. I did everything I could think of to get her off my mind. Started playing tennis again, threw myself into church work—of all things—but it wasn't enough.

I started calling her, desperate, miserably unhappy, and she just laughed at me. She said the straight life was marvelous, maybe I ought to try marriage counseling or sex therapy. I wanted to scream.

Then I remembered the pictures. We were in a loft in the Village for three days—bombed out on grass and 'ludes, not giving a damn if the sun came up. Afterward, my photographer friend gave me a stack of negatives as a memento. These are part of them.

She didn't know I had them, but you can bet she listened the next time I called. Now she sends a nice little check every month, regular as clockwork; I only had to remind her twice, so far.

I don't need the money; it's just nice to have the feeling I can crush that double-dealing bitch anytime I want to.

I know this has probably shocked you and I'm sorry; if only you'd paid more attention to me back then, it might have come out differently. You know how much I love you.

But, it doesn't really make any difference now, does it?

Good-bye, dear Bobby
Laura

"Dick, now you know why I sounded so down on the phone last night."

"I sure do. It's an awfully depressing story. A sad, lost child who never grew up. Break the toy rather than let someone else play with it. A sorry, sorry business indeed."

He turned to Bassett and Hampton. "Gentlemen, I think it's high time Mr. MacCardle and I got out of the middle of this. If I may be so bold, let me suggest you make a print of those revolting pictures, then take them, the bankbook, and the letter over to Elaine Paley and confront her with them."

"While you're at it," I added, "ask her where she was Wednesday night, when Bobby Evans was murdered. She just might turn out to be the phantom reporter the Ormond Beach police are trying to find."

Hampton, of course, had the last word. "Mr. MacCardle, you are either one of the smartest or luckiest people I know, not that it makes much of a difference which. Mr. Ellis, I know you'll believe me when I say those thoughts were going through my mind while you were talking. We will, indeed, pay a call on Mrs. Paley, as quick as the lab boys can process a set of prints. We're still going to hold onto your client, Counselor, but I have a hunch it won't be for long. Thank you for your time, Mr. Bassett. I know I can count on you to keep this confidential for now. If you'll excuse me, all, I've got a job to do."

The Pelican's Roost never looked so good. The pleasant-faced waitress was glad to see us and kept the drinks and munchies flowing in a steady stream. The bartender, a prince of a chap, threw in one on the house every third round. Susan had to come down and drive Dick home. As for me—the free and happy bachelor—Cooney's Cab Company did the honors, having the good sense to send me a driver who could sing. "Oh, no, 'twas the light in her eyes ever shining, that made me love Mary, the Rose of Tralee."

M.E. would have loved it.

21

"The lab technicians had the prints done by six," Dick told us. "Hampton and Serkin went straight to the Las Olas house. Got there right in the middle of a monster cocktail party and sent a maid in to fetch Mrs. Paley. She came out friendly as could be, according to Hampton, said she'd be glad to help in any way, took them into a little study downstairs. Asked them if she could get them anything to drink. They said no thanks; it really wasn't a social visit. Showed her the bankbook, the pictures, and the letter. Hampton expected a big reaction from her but didn't get it. He said she simply mumbled something about God's will, and asked him what was going to happen next.

"The lawyer had already arrived when they took her in for questioning—Forrest Paley had seen to that. Good man too. Sam Barker, year ahead of me at Stetson. He was with her for the whole session, kept advising her she didn't have to answer any questions, not to volunteer any information. Hampton said she paid no attention at all to Sam, the words pouring out of her as if she were glad to be getting rid of them. The telling took three hours, but then you guys probably know most of it by now."

We were sitting in my breakfast room on a Saturday morning, three weeks after our meeting with Bassett and Hampton. Dick had suggested we get together. I'd provided home and coffee; the assortment of Dunkin Donuts was Billy's contribution. The local media *had* been running wild with the Elaine Paley story. She was bigger than OPEC, bigger than the recession, even bigger than the record unemployment level Florida was suffering.

"All we know is what we read in the papers, Counselor. You be the judge of how accurate those guys are. Isn't it about time you told us what's really going on?"

"Uh-huh. That's why I called. But you got to keep this under your hats. It'll all come out next week, but for now it's ultraconfidential. Hampton took a hell of a chance giving me a copy of her transcript; we can't let him down. I'm going to read the highlights of it to you in her words, rather than transposing it into 'she saids and she dids,' if that's all right with you two."

"C'mon, already!"

Dick pulled his glasses on, opened the bound transcript, and began:

"She phoned me to say the price of silence had just gone up. From now on it was two thousand dollars a month or else certain people were going to get the shock of their lives. I was panic-stricken. A thousand dollars a month was hard enough to hide in the household expenses; two thousand would be impossible. Besides, where would it go from there? I had to see her, had to try to talk her out of it, to find out what I ever could have done to make her hate me so. She finally agreed to see me at her house Monday afternoon. Monday the thirteenth—I won't forget that date soon.

"I got over there shortly before four. She met me at the door barefoot, in a bathrobe, with a drink in her hand—obviously not the first of the day from the look of her.

"She'd remembered I drank vodka and tonic and had one waiting for me, which I accepted, like a damn fool. I don't drink well, and besides I wanted to keep my wits about me, even if she didn't care.

"But I was nervous enough to drink it and to ask for another as we talked. I found myself reminiscing about the old days, how much we'd meant to each other, and realized I was crying.

"She said it was taking longer than she'd thought, that we

needed more time alone together. I wasn't quite sure what she meant, but it was *her* meeting. She picked up the phone, called Dreary Ralph—at his office, I guess—and gave him some incredible cock-and-bull story I swear she made up on the spot. Quite a job of acting and I told her so. She said he was so dim he believed anything she said, and that now we had all the time we needed."

"Excuse me, Dick," I interrupted. "What if Dim and Dreary hadn't bought her act? Supposing he'd decided to pass, then what?"

"Probably wouldn't have changed the eventual outcome. They hadn't resolved anything yet. They would have just set up another time. If Ralph checked with his friend, Laura could always have played innocent, claimed she was just passing along a message."

"Yeah, with no way of proving she made the whole thing up. Go on, please."

He picked up the narrative again.

"The third drink really hit me. Maybe Laura loaded it, maybe it was my small capacity, but I knew I was suddenly far from sober. As we talked, Laura's bathrobe came more and more undone. I realized she had nothing on underneath. Despite myself, it excited me.

"She must have noticed I was staring at her. She stood up and smiled at me—that shy, pretty smile of hers—undid the robe, and walked over to me. 'This is what you really want, isn't it, Pookie,' she said, 'this is what you always want. Come on, Pookie. Let's go to our island.'

"I followed her upstairs, like a robot, knowing it was wrong, somehow no longer able to resist. I got undressed, took her into my arms, made love on the same bed she shared with that dreary little man. Afterward, she snuggled up to me, told me in a sleepy, little-girl voice she thought she'd take a nap, and would I wake her in an hour for more. She pointed to a framed picture on her dresser and said if I had any funny ideas to just forget it, she had permanent insurance. Then she turned over and went to sleep.

"I almost had a heart attack when I heard the front door open. I'd forgotten Laura had said something about Ralph coming by to pick up the briefcase she put in the hall, after she'd finished talking to him.

"Apparently, he was in quite a hurry. I heard him say 'Laura? Laura, it's me. Where are you?' I lay there holding my breath, wondering where to hide if he came upstairs. Then I heard him curse; the next thing I heard was the door slamming as he left.

"I got up, went to the bathroom, caught sight of myself in the full-length mirror on the back of the door. I realized what I'd done, and I hated myself for it. I knew I would do it again, any time she offered, knew there was no end as long as she lived.

"I went back into the bedroom and looked down at her—sleeping, all innocence, her arms at her sides, breasts rising and falling as she breathed.

"I straddled her—quickly, gently so as not to wake her up—pinning her wrists to the bed with my knees. She stirred and grumbled, but slept on. Maybe she was more intoxicated than I thought. I reached over, got the big bed pillow, put it over her face—pushing as hard as I could, keeping it there until I felt her breathing stop. I pulled the pillow away and forced myself to look at her. It wasn't a pretty face anymore. It was almost purple. I remember thinking I couldn't take the chance she might recover when I was gone, so I took the sash off her bathrobe and knotted it around her neck with all the strength I had left. Her tongue . . . popped out . . . hideous.

"I put Laura in the middle of the bed, smoothed out the covers, and replaced the pillow. Then I remembered she'd said something about insurance; the framed picture had something to do with insurance.

"I went over and got it off her dresser—a picture of her brother in a race-car driver's suit, holding a helmet under his arm, squinting into the sun. I wondered what she meant by 'insurance,' what had made her so smug, so sure of herself. She wouldn't have told her brother about us, *couldn't* have, not and keep up her lovely little image.

"I knew I couldn't take the picture with me—surely even that oaf Ralph would remember it when the police started investigating—and I knew I had to leave— I *wanted* to get out of there in the worst way imaginable. In frustration, I smashed the picture against a corner of the dresser. There was glass all over the place. And something else, hidden behind the picture—a smallish envelope.

"When I picked it up and tore it open, out came six of those horrible prints she'd been threatening me with. I thought, that isn't much of an insurance policy; I can take care of that in a hurry. I wiped the broken picture frame with a corner of the bedspread and put it back on the floor where it would look as if it simply got knocked off the dresser by accident. I knew I had to leave quickly—while there was time enough—and I still had to get rid of any trace of my having been there.

"Suddenly, I realized what a twist of providence Ralph Morgan represented. He hadn't seen me, didn't know I was there. But I knew he had been home and was off on a fruitless, time-consuming venture. Let him be the one the police accused. What perfect irony. And to think Laura caused it all—her own death and his paying for it.

"I got dressed, went downstairs, and stuffed the pictures into my purse. I took our glasses, emptied them, put them in the dishwasher, and turned it on to the full cycle setting. I wiped everything I could remember touching with some paper toweling from the kitchen. I put on my driving gloves and let myself out the kitchen door, then walked around the darkened back of their unit to the visitors parking lot.

"I drove home, went up to my bathroom, burned the pictures, flushed the ashes down the toilet. I joined Forrie for dinner at eight. He asked me what kind of a day I had had."

"She must have thought she was pretty safe," I said, "particularly when the police nominated Ralph the one and only fall guy. After all, she knew where he was at the time and knew he'd have a helluva time getting anyone to believe him. Then I bumble by and confirm that poor old Ralph can't substantiate any part of his story and ask for her help; it's a wonder she didn't start giggling. Yessir, guys, Cam MacCardle, intrepid sleuth and keen judge of character—idiot's delight would be more like it."

"You didn't lack for company, Cam. She fooled all of us—Ralph, husband, police, the whole lot. Among her other talents, Elaine turned out to be a first-rate actress."

"I *guess*. I'd have followed her anywhere. What I don't understand is why she had to kill Bobby Evans. Ralph was all set up, the cops were totally satisfied; she must have thought she was home free."

"Yes and no. She did feel safe at first, according to the transcript. Then she began to worry more and more about what Laura meant in talking about insurance—whether the prints she destroyed were, in fact, all that was involved. But let's get it in her own words."

"The prints had been burned—I knew that—I took care of it myself. I still didn't believe that Laura had told her brother about us; it simply wasn't her way. But maybe those weren't all the prints. Worse yet, where there are prints there must be negatives to make them from. I had to get those or the whole thing could flare up again.

"Everything pointed to Bobby Evans. I mean, that was the only logical answer. Laura's insurance policy had to be more than a handful of prints. Maybe Bobby was involved, maybe Laura had sent something to him for safekeeping, maybe he didn't even know what he had, maybe he was totally ignorant—maybe, maybe, maybe . . . .

"All I knew was I couldn't take the risk of doing nothing. I had to see him as quickly as possible, had to find out what he knew, even if—God willing—it was nothing. I'd obviously have to figure out what to say to him. Meantime, the first job was deciding how and where, so that no one would know if things went badly.

"I thought he lived in South Carolina—Greenville, South Carolina. He had when I'd met him at Laura's wedding; hopefully he still did. But how to get to him without making him suspicious? How to make sure nothing could go wrong, no matter what?

"Then I remembered all the time I spent giving interviews to the press. It's all a big bore, but you simply have to do it. Athletes must go through the same thing.

"I went to my bookstore—it has magazines on every subject of interest you can name. There were four on stock-car racing. I picked the one that looked as if it were written by rednecks—mostly pictures and quotes, no technical slant to it at all. *Motor Sports Illustrated*, a tabloid-size newspaper. I had fun making up a name for my reporter impersonation; finally decided Denise Conway had the right ring to it.

"I got his Greenville number from directory assistance and started calling him right after we got back from Nassau. He kept putting me off, saying he was too busy to see me. I was getting frantic. At last I threatened him, said I was going to write a story on him one way or another. How would it look to the fans if I wrote that he wouldn't talk to the press anymore?

"He finally agreed to let me buy him dinner at Daytona, Wednesday the twenty-seventh. I said I would call to confirm. He gave me a number there where he could be reached.

"I told Forrie I'd be gone overnight, on the campaign, two Women's Club speeches and a testimonial dinner—I'd done that several times before legitimately, so it wasn't anything out of the ordinary.

"I drove up to Daytona Wednesday morning, went on through to the town next to it, Ormond Beach. Found a seedy-looking motel there, so close to the road the lobby shook when the big trucks went by. I rented a room under the name Conway for two nights and paid cash in advance to avoid identification questions. I had on a straw cowboy hat to hide my hair, sunglasses, and a jeans suit I'd picked up on the way. *I* wouldn't have known me.

"I called, left the false name and my room number, and asked the man to have Bobby pick me up at seven. When I opened the door to let him in he must have been the most surprised man in Florida—seeing me instead of some reporter, standing there pointing a gun at him. I have a little thirty-two automatic Forrie got me to keep in the car for when I'm riding around. At first I didn't want any part of it, but Forrie convinced me, showed me how to fire the thing, and now I feel comfortable with it.

"Pardon me? Oh, yes, what happened next with Bobby Evans? Sorry.

"I motioned him into the room and had him sit on a chair with his back to me, hands on the chair's arms where I could see them. He was terribly upset, of course, kept asking me what was going on.

"On the drive up I'd decided I had to kill him; it was really the only solution. I hadn't been able to come up with a line of questions for him that would tell me what I had to know. I mean, you don't simply ask, 'By the way, did Laura send you or give you anything I should know about?' There just wasn't any way to find out without linking me to Laura's murder, and I knew I couldn't stand up under any kind of police investigation. Bobby must have sensed something too, and began to turn just before I hit him on the head with the gun butt, as hard as I knew how, holding it by the barrel for leverage. He tumbled out of the chair, still breathing but unconscious on the floor.

"I horsed him up onto the bed, put the gun just under his ear—at the chin line, pointing upward—put a pillow over it to muffle the sound. I waited for a passing truck; when it came I pulled the trigger. I waited for another truck and fired once more to make sure.

"I pulled the gun out, surprised how little blood was on my hand; evidently it all went in the other direction. I washed my hands, rinsed the basin, dried my hands on my jeans.

"I put the room key in my purse, left the motel, drove south to Melbourne, and spent the night there, in another anonymous place, still under the false name, cash on the barrelhead, no questions asked.

"Before I went to bed I walked all the way out to the end of a long fishing pier next door and threw the key and the gun as far out into the ocean as I could. I stuffed the jeans suit in a Goodwill box in Vero Beach the next day on my way home.

"I got back just after noon, called Forrie to check in, told him everything had gone well, that I'd see him at suppertime.

"I suppose I should have been relieved, but I wasn't. Somehow, I knew those pictures would show up again, that the nightmare would begin once more. I didn't think they'd show up quite so soon.

"I'm glad it's over. I couldn't live with what I did, or with what I had become.

"Sorry? You ask me if I'm sorry? Certainly, I'm sorry. Sorry for Mama and Daddy, for Forrie and all the people who believed in me. Sorry for what might have been, what should have been. Most of all, I'm sorry I ever met Laura Evans. She was like a dangerous drug to me, something illegal and immoral, fascinating by its wickedness, totally addictive. I couldn't stay away from her, then or ever. She was *me*, I was *her*.

"Now she's killed us both."

I remembered a girl from my college days crying in my arms, wanting to freeze time, unwilling, unable to look ahead, anticipating that the future could not be more pleasant than what she had already known. Would that it were that easy. Would that the two friends could begin again—and this time get things right.

I knew it couldn't happen, that what was done was done. There would be no new start, no changes possible, no happy ending. As if she were beside me, I could hear my aunt Fiona quoting another of a seemingly endless string of Scottish poets, seeking in her way to understand and move ahead:

> For a' the living of our days,
> For a' the errors of our ways,
> For a' the deeds we should have done,
> Forgie us Lord.
> Nae that we're gone.

Here's wishing that He does, Aunt Fee.

Billy broke the silence. "Dick, what will happen to Elaine Paley when all this comes out in the trial?"

"Death warrant would be my guess. They might have been able to plea bargain Laura's murder. Crime of passion, temporary insanity, that kind of thing. But, Bobby Evans's killing changes the whole picture. Premeditated murder, as painstakingly plotted as that was, is pretty tough for a jury to gloss over. She might get off with a life sentence, but I doubt it. The concern over the crime rate these days, exploitation by the media, public pressure on the judicial system—just too much to overcome. She'll probably go through the whole process of appeals and stays and so forth—might drag on as much as five or six years, if current practices prevail. Bottom line? My bet is she'll pay for it with her life.

"Maybe worst of all, she'll have all the time between now and whenever to relive what she did, without being able to change a single part of it. God grant her the strength to face those days, perhaps even to come to peace with herself."

"Trust you to see that side of it, Billy," I said. "But we've left out the hero of the piece. What do you hear from Mr. Excitement these days?"

"Don't be too hard on Ralph. He's just an average little man who got caught in the middle. He called me ten days ago. He's put the condominium up for sale and asked his company to transfer him. Anywhere. He said he had to get away—too many bad memories here, too much to live with. He wants to start over somewhere else, try to forget, though I'm sure he never will."

"He still doesn't know the whole story," I said. "Neither do we, come to think of it. Someone played house with her Monday afternoon, but who? Not Ralph, not that Kenny kid, and for sure it wasn't Dear Dana. Maybe she had a thing for the postman. Not that it makes any difference now. I sure thought it was a biggie at the time, though."

From Dick: "On a somewhat lighter note, Cam, what are you going to do now? Back to the life of the idle rich?"

"Not so loud, Counselor. Smollert probably has the joint bugged for sound. The guys in New York keep after me; I got another letter last week. They want me to be their Southeast regional scout, travel around, look at the local talent. The money isn't much, but it sure beats watching the tube."

"Well, okay, if that's what you want to do. I have a reason for asking, however. I think you did a more than competent job of digging, certainly much more than we asked you to do. I need that kind of help more or less constantly—more on that in a minute or so—and as they say, better a devil you know. . . . We can set up some kind of per diem compensation, which our clients can more than afford; that way we both get something out of it.

"Case in point. The Wentworth family—the old man was the headache tablet king—are apparently short one heiress. Name of Lisa. Last known whereabouts was Lago Mar, outside Jacksonville. They want us to locate her so she can sign some powers of attorney on her voting stock. Simple job and at least a change of pace from this dreadful affair. Would you at least think about it, Cam?"

"Sure. Not much going on this time of year except spring training, which is about as exciting as watching cement set. The screwy part of this Morgan thing was I found I really enjoyed it—frustrations, dead ends, and wild-goose chases notwithstanding. At least I felt I was doing something worthwhile, particularly the way it turned out, and it sure as hell wasn't boring. Lago Mar isn't exactly Howard Johnson's either; better class of people than present company. I have a couple of things to do this afternoon—maybe we could talk some more about it tonight."

"Good man. C'mon, Billy, you've got to get me home to free up Susan for grocery shopping. Don't forget, gents, the cookout starts at six. Bring your best appetites; Susan's starting with oyster stew."

"S'long, Cam, gotta play chauffeur. See you later."

I sat trying to think of the words of summary. Somehow, "all's well that ends well" didn't make the grade.

I was pleased to see Ralph Morgan cleared of something he hadn't done. The little don't always lose. In the end justice really had been served.

Perhaps my world was yet too black and white. 'Nam should have taught you that, dummy. There aren't any good guys and bad guys anymore. Only people, scurrying around, trying to survive in a world they can't control.

22

My two pieces of business to deal with in the afternoon were *both* pleasant, for a refreshing change.

After Ralph Morgan's release and Elaine Paley's indictment, Hampton had called Phillip Corwin, knowing who he was, to give Corwin the final resolution of the case involving his daughter's death. Mercifully, not many details had reached the New York media; hopefully, they never would.

Shortly after that, I received a nice letter of gratitude from Mr. Corwin, including a certified check for fifty thousand dollars. Dick, Billy, and I had debated what to do with the money, including sending it back, but finally settled on what we thought would be its most appropriate use.

Time to communicate that news to Phillip Corwin. I, worst of correspondents, was chosen to be the communicator. I tried to close the loop gracefully. I told him about the debate and our eventual solution, knowing, somehow, that he would understand.

> . . . We set up a joint trust arrangement with the Juilliard School of Music. Each year, in perpetuity, the interest earned by the trust will be used to help offset tuition costs of that student Juilliard believes to be the most deserving.
>
> Without consulting you, I'm afraid, we've named it the Laura Corwin Scholarship.
>
> Sincerely,
> A. Cameron MacCardle

Having finished the letter, I paused to think over what Dick had said about my long-range plans—"career wise," the words of Madison Avenue. I'd only gotten involved because of Billy. Hampton said I was the luckiest person he'd ever met and I couldn't quarrel with that, granted the circumstances. Maybe the whole thing would have worked out without me. Whoa, there, doubting Angus, be fair to yourself. You did a much better job than you thought you could, certainly good enough to have Dick want to use you again. And you did enjoy it, didn't you? C'mon, don't kid yourself. A missing heiress? An expense-account shot at the high-rent district. You got something better to do?

In any event it would have to wait until the middle of March. No matter what.

When I had finally come home from the New York/Daytona/Greenville jaunt, there was a fearsome stack of accumulated mail lying helter-skelter in my foyer. As I sorted through it, I came across a small gray envelope, handwritten in a graceful backhand. The upper-left-hand corner identified the author:

Phelan, Apt.1D
356 East 72nd Street
New York, New York.

Now I crossed to the desk, reopened the note, read it for a second time.

Dear Cam,

We were talking about famous wastrels the other day and your name came up.

I seem to remember some line of guff involving a guest room and a pool, place called Lighthouse Point. The guy swore he owned it, too. Big, ugly guy. Named MacCardle, I believe. He said come down any old time, just give him a little notice. I hope he wasn't just putting me on.

I have a week's vacation, starting March 1. I'm terrible at skiing and I've had enough snow to last me forever, anyway.

A little sunshine would be wonderful, not to mention the fringe benefits.

   If it fits your plans, please call me. You can usually get me at home, afternoons. The number is 212-555-3074.

   If it doesn't fit your plans, I'll have you arrested and extradited.

Love,
M.E.

   I put the letter down, picked up the phone, and called the New York number. We talked for at least a half hour—probably get a heart attack when that phone bill comes in, I thought.

   Finally, I hung up, still laughing.

   I called Ellis.

   "Dick, can little Miss Wentworth wait until after the eighth?"

   "She's been gone for better than two months, Cam; another week won't make that much difference. Any particular reason for the delay?"

   "Seminar in community–police relations."

   "Good for you. Of course you should attend. Probably be a real help to you in the future. Those things always are. Promoting mutual cooperation and goodwill, eh?"

   "Close enough, Counselor."